Bolan swept the M-16 in a stuttering arc

The five airboats detonated in rapid-fire, ripping the air apart. An oily ball of flame consumed men and their machines with fine impartiality.

Two of the airboats collided, one climbing onto the deck of the other, fan blades clashing and disintegrating. A driver drenched in gasoline fell flaming into the firelit water.

Then one of the giant fans spun free of its restraining cage, and the whirling blade was hurled through space like a giant lethal Frisbee....

D0720812

Other
MACK BOLAN
titles in the Gold Eagle
Executioner series

Mack Bolan's
ABLE TEAM

Mack Bolan's
PHOENIX FORCE

MACK

THE EXECUTIONER 45

BOLAN

Paramilitary Plot

DON PENDLETON

A GOLD EAGLE BOOK FROM

W RLDWIDE

TORONTO • NEW YORK • LOS ANGELES • LONDON

First edition September 1982

ISBN 0-373-61045-9

Special thanks and acknowledgment to
Mike Newton for his contributions to this work.

Printed in Canada

The pleasure of hating makes patriotism
an excuse for carrying fire, pestilence and
famine into other lands...
                              —*William Hazlitt*

Fanaticism consists of redoubling your effort
when you have forgotten your aim.
                              —*George Santayana*

If we lose sight of our aims and join the
enemy in cultivating the pleasure of hatred,
then we are already defeated and there is
no place left in the world for the noble heart.
                              —*Mack Bolan*
                              (from the Phoenix journal)

Dedicated to the brave and persistent police officers of Italy who gave us back our Southern NATO Commander, Gen. Bill Dozier.

Well done. Stay hard.

PROLOGUE

An ugly monster that would have worked well in a Hollywood horror movie filled the electronic screen in the Stony Man war room. Bolan stared at it with fascination for a moment before responding audibly. "That's the bug?"

"That's the one," April confirmed. "Magnified a whole bunch of times, of course. Enough of these microscopic monsters to infect a major American city could be packed into a thimble."

Brognola added, "Assuming, of course, that you could get them out of the thimble and somehow spread into the atmosphere. Otherwise you'd have your standard epidemic situation, spreading slowly from victim to victim by direct contact."

"This isn't a standard CBW agent, then," Bolan decided.

"Not the usual variety, no," Brognola said. "This damn thing produces an effect very similar to bubonic plague. The people at CDC would not have noticed the difference if we hadn't insisted on a closer rundown." He gently nudged the operations chief and requested, "Let's see that morgue shot again, April."

The pretty lady worked a combination at the console to recall an earlier file. The four-times-larger-than-life photo of a nude male rippled onto the screen. First guess would place the victim as a member of the black race. But it was the body of a male Caucasian, age 45, one Stuart Dunlop, Special Agent for the FBI.

In a barely audible voice, April pointed out, "That dark discoloration of the flesh is typical in these cases. Note also the localized swelling in the groin and armpit areas. These bugs love lymph glands."

Brognola made a face at that. "Not a very sweet romance for the victim, I'd say."

"Nearly always fatal," April murmured. "Decimated populations in Europe and Asia during the 14th century."

"Why would anyone want to bring it back?" Bolan said quietly.

"That's what we're hoping you'll tell us," Brognola replied.

"How do you know it didn't happen naturally?" Bolan wondered. "That whole area down there is swarming with refugees. This could be a full-scale medical problem. Dunlop could have picked up the bug somewhere. What was he working on?''

''Let's have the next file, April.''

The operations chief did her thing at the keyboard. The darkened corpse of FBI Agent Dunlop faded away, to be replaced by the troubled likeness of a slight man in his fifties. The hair was thinning, sandy colored, carelessly coiffed. A string of foot-high words began forming beneath the photo, describing the subject. This was one William Bruce, biochemist, chief of biochemical research for *Warco*, an energy conglomerate. Age 51, widower, a daughter Holly presently attending Florida State University. Eminent scientist, on and off consultant to the U.S. government, twice considered for Nobels, unquestioned loyalty, a man of quiet habits and low public profile.

''Okay,'' Bolan commented softly. ''I'll buy him.''

''Who wouldn't?'' Brognola responded. ''And who wouldn't try to?''

''That the problem?''

''Maybe. His daughter has reported him as a missing person. Apparently the employer in Tampa is at odds with the daughter. Warco says that their chief of research is on a well-deserved vacation. The local authorities are buying that. The girl is not. She's downright frantic, now, calling everyone in Washington she can get through to. Justice even had an inquiry from the National Academy of Science." Brognola frowned. "The girl just lost her mother two years ago. Maybe. . . ."

"How long has he been gone?"

"Three weeks."

"It's a pretty thin connection, Hal. A biochemist, okay. A virulent bacillus, okay. One's missing and one's been discovered. But that's not necessarily. . . ."

Brognola sighed and reached for a cigar. "Well, you see, that's what Dunlop was working on. Very quietly, understand, just a routine inquiry into the facts. To placate the pressures brought by the daughter."

Bolan said, "Okay, so there could be a connection. Let's have the rest of it, pal. Don't cat and mouse me. I'm tired and I'm grouchy and I've got Phoenix Force and Able fighting a couple of pretty hot fires right now. Where'd they find Dunlop?"

"Apparently he drove himself to a hospital in Ft. Myers. Checked himself in. Told the emergency room doctor he thought he'd been exposed to a toxic agent. But he was already very sick and practically incoherent. Died an hour later."

Another photo was rippling onto the screen. "This one just became available," April announced. "Could be interesting, Striker. Take a look."

Bolan stared soberly at the screen as the picture took shape. It was a very lovely young lady, early twenties, blonde, a hint of devilish delight in the eyes.

"Holly Bruce," April explained. "Sorry, no personal details. We tapped this from the college files. Very attractive."

She certainly was. Bolan stared at the photo for a long, quiet moment. Brognola lit his cigar. Holly Bruce took her departure, replaced by her father. April said, all business again, "This man has worked on army CBW projects on three separate occassions over the past twenty years. He is regarded as one of the leading authorities on the manipulation of virulent biological strains. The bug we were looking at a moment ago has definitely been manipulated. It has a genetic structure similar to, yet tantalizingly distinct from, the bubonic bacillus. It's like has never before been recorded in any laboratory in the Western world. The genetic structure is such that it may—now I say *may*—it *may* be vectored as a standard chemical warfare agent yet experienced as a natural disease. Our own people know nothing of this structure but they'd surely like to.''

"What is *Warco*?'' Bolan grunted.

April replied, ''Petroleum, banking, utilities, chemicals, recently bought a couple of small computer firms. The plaything of the one and only Thurston Ward, megamillionaire, patron of the reactionary political arts.''

"I've heard of him.''

"Who hasn't? This is the man who accused Billy Graham of idolatry.''

Brognola chuckled. Bolan pushed back, lit a cigarette. "I guess it's no laughing matter, is it?'' he said after a moment. "We have all the ingredients here for a real barn burner. Guess I better get down there. Show me the girl again, April.''

The "girl'' reappeared as if by magic.

Bolan stared at her for another long moment. "Lost her momma, too,'' he commented quietly.

"God but he's a sucker for a pretty face,'' April said in mock disgust.

"For yours, only, my lady,'' Bolan assured her gallantly. But he had been moved, yes, by that pretty face upon the screen. It reminded him of another that had not been allowed to quite reach that maturity, a face that had launched young Mack Bolan into war unremitting.

"Looks a little like my kid sister," he added.

April said, "oh," and cast a stricken glance at Brognola.

But Bolan did not see that. He was already up and moving toward the next mission. The Executioner was en route to the Florida Everglades.

When Mack Bolan retired from his private war against the Mafia, he did so with a purpose. The thought of rest and relaxation, so alluring to a battle-weary warrior, never seriously crossed his mind. Instead, he resigned his role in one conflict to join another—a new war, against a threat more insidious than any ever offered by the mob.

Terror was a chief target in Bolan's newest phase of war everlasting. In a world divided on the lines of race, ideology, religion, the firebrands and fanatics found a fertile breeding ground. For too many years, small bands of savages, often acting without coherent thought or guiding policy, had held the world at bay. Free nations often seemed powerless to stem the violent tide.

Time for Mack Bolan.

Or, rather, time for "John Phoenix," a full

colonel in America's *sub rosa* war against the terrorists.

The Bolan identity had for all intents and purposes been shed in the final hours of his "last mile" against the Mafia. As a fugitive and public figure, the Executioner was "dead."

But the man, *the real man*, was still very much alive. Still breathing, thinking, caring.

And still fighting.

He had learned many things in the early days of his new war. Not least among those lessons was the fact that terrorism is a universal evil. Despite the urge to generalize, to point a finger, he had learned that no country, no creed, no cause held a firm monopoly on terror. Anywhere, any time that public discontent erupts in violence, there was room for the seed of terror to sprout and send down greedy roots, sucking out the lives of innocent men, women and children.

Nor was terrorism an exclusive province of the alien, the foreigner. Domestic madmen were as lethal as any import, and often more destructive to the nation which they claimed to cherish and defend.

It was ironic, thought Bolan, that through its laws, which were the very safeguards designed to nurture liberty and freedom of expression, America had grown into an unwitting haven for the enemies of freedom. They had come in many guises through the years: nativists and racists, nightriders and homegrown "liberation armies," bombers of banks and synagogues. But they were all the same in their effect.

The domestic terrorists concealed themselves in ways that foreigners could never hope to emulate, merging with the population, cloaking themselves in the system which they sought to topple, boring from within. They would pervert the laws and Constitution, hiding in the chinks and loopholes like a lethal breed of parasite.

When the laws were twisted and abused to shield the murderers, when their subtle threat became a clear and present danger, it was time for some direct and forceful counteraction.

Time for men like Mack Bolan.

And that was another lesson for the Executioner: the message that his latest struggle wasn't such a new one, after all. Certainly, the names had changed, and the faces. The field of battle might be anywhere, the target any man. But at bottom, in the deep living heart of things, it was all the same war, everywhere.

Civilized Man, the builder, versus Savage Man, the destroyer.

It was a war with roots in Cain and Abel, branches in Biafra, Belfast, Vietnam. War everlasting, yeah.

Mack Bolan had signed on for the duration, and while strength—while life itself—remained, he would continue the fight.

Because he cared.

1

The warrior crouched inside a black, inflatable boat, urging it along the winding waterway with powerful strokes of a short aluminum paddle. He hugged the shoreline, using it for cover, every combat sense alert to the sights and sounds of the swampland around him. It was mid-morning, and warm, but the sunlight was screened and mottled by stands of palmettos and cypress and water tupelos. Beneath the trees lay a world of shadow. And in shadows there was danger.

All of Mack Bolan's adult life had been spent in one sort of jungle or another, and he knew jungles well. He had learned his martial craft in the steaming rain forests of the Orient, then came home to practice it in the underworld jungles of his native land. He was familiar with the predators in every sort of jungle habitat. Like his human enemies, they were each unique, and yet in many ways were all the same.

He found the Everglades to be a place of striking contrasts, with teeming life played off against the lurking, ever-present threat of death. Neutral rather than hostile, the marshland played no favorites with man or animal. One misstep, and the unwary traveler was swallowed up alive.

The swamp was a microcosm of the universe, with all the laws of predator and prey in strict effect. Here, survival of the fittest had been perfected to the status of a living art form.

And behind the startling blend of beauty and monotony, stagnation and rebirth, lay a pervasive undercurrent of menace. Danger. Nothing was quite what it appeared to be. Nothing could be taken at face value. The delicate clustered blossoms of the swamp sumac were laden with a deadly poison nectar. Graceful carnivorous plants lured insects to their doom with fragrant sweetness. Swamp roses bloomed above a quicksand bog disguised as solid ground. A twisted root or branch, festooned with flowers, was in fact a deadly cottonmouth, poised to strike.

The swampland was a predatory place, and Bolan, the hunter, felt right at home there.

He nosed the black rubber boat in beneath the cover of some vines and branches drooping to the water level. Nearby, a log sprouted eyes and became an alligator, disappearing underwater with a single sweep of its powerful armored tail. Bolan checked his surroundings for other hazards, then secured his craft to some roots with a nylon line, scrambling out and onto the bank. The rest of his journey would be made on foot.

He was rigged for jungle combat, dressed in camouflage fatigues, the Beretta Brigadier with silencer in its holster underneath his left arm, the big silver AutoMag riding military web at his right hip. Bolan's lead weapon was an M-16 assault rifle in the carbine configuration. With its shorter barrel and telescoping stock, the rifle was ideal for close-range jungle warfare, retaining all the stunning firepower of the full-sized original. Bolan had beefed up the M-16's capability by adding an outsized drum magazine; the drum held seventy-five of the deadly 5.56mm tumblers, giving him an immediate advantage over any foe he was likely to encounter on his mission. He carried extra clips for all the weapons on his combat harness, along with strangulation gear, grenades, and a K-Bar fighting knife.

Bolan was rigged for battle, yes, but this was supposed to be a soft and silent probe. A simple reconnaissance mission. Any premature contact with the enemy would jeopardize the mission, and court the risk of possible disaster.

His target was a paramilitary compound carved out of the living swamp. Bolan approached from the west, circling it silently, invisibly, scanning its layout and defenses before settling down to a secure observation post along the southernmost perimeter.

Surrounded by brackish water on the north and east, by jungle on the south and west, the compound was roughly one hundred meters on a side, bounded by a tall chain-link fence topped by razor wire. Around the main gate, and along the land-side fence, the undergrowth had been cut back to a distance of about thirty meters, creating a field of fire in case the occupants were forced to become defenders. But those occupants had grown careless with time, secure in the knowledge of their isolation, and in spots the jungle was again encroaching on the wire.

Bolan kept to the shadows, moving frequently, skirting the perimeter and scanning the compound's corrugated metal buildings. From one, he heard the hum of diesel engines, and the tentacles of insulated cable radiating from the roof identified a generator hut. Sentries were visible, walking their posts, decked out in camouflage fatigues with M-16s slung over muscular shoulders, eyes alert and probing at the jungle just outside the wire.

And the word that came to mind was *professional*.

Other men, uniformed and wearing side arms, were visible from time to time, moving in and out among the buildings on various errands, some of them carrying manila folders or armloads of equipment. Nowhere was there any sign of the man Mack Bolan had come so far to locate.

And he kept moving, scanning, searching.

On the north, where land sloped away into stagnant water, half a dozen airboats were tethered to the shore. Bolan marked their presence, filing it away for future reference. He knew the fan-driven, flat-bottomed airboats gave his enemy mobility which he himself did not possess, but there were drawbacks, too. At need, the seeming advantage might be turned around, converted into a telling weapon against the hardsite occupants.

Bolan found the compound professionally built, as well as manned. Nearly invisible from the air, it would be easy to miss even from land and water level. Penetration of the camp would be a risky proposition, clearly, but not impossible. For safety's sake, it would have to wait for dark.

The Executioner was finishing his second circuit of the compound, already working back in the direction of his hidden boat, when a stealthy movement in among the trees alerted him to danger. Human movement, yes, to be sure. He wondered if a roving sentinel had stumbled on his track, or if the guy was simply scouring the perimeter along his normal beat.

Either way, Bolan meant to be prepared.

He slid the Beretta from its armpit sheath, melting into shadow, taking aim. In the murky light, he saw a figure of less than average height, dressed in O.D. green, a knit cap pulled low over brow and ears. The person appeared to be unarmed, certainly he was without the military rigging the other sentries wore in common. Still, this person was following Bolan's trail with a precision that ruled out coincidences—and sealed the little guy's fate.

Too late, the figure hesitated, freezing, head craned forward. Narrowed eyes were straining in the half-light, finally making the connection, and then the guy was turning, taking to his heels, breaking for the cover of the trees.

Bolan's finger tightened on the trigger. It would be an easy shot at thirty yards. One gentle squeeze, and. . . .

He hesitated. There was something about the tracker, something in his slight stature and uncertain attitude, which made Bolan question that person's affiliation with the hardsite. His suspicion was confirmed at once, as the figure turned and ran away from the compound, deeper into the swamp, instead of toward the fence and waiting sentries.

Bolan made his decision in the space of a heartbeat. Leaping from cover, he pursued the little guy on foot, running with a silent speed born of long conditioning. Ahead of him, lean and agile, his quarry was making good time, but with his longer legs and greater stamina, Bolan quickly closed the gap.

And he kept the Beretta ready in his fist, just in case.

The undergrowth was closing in, growing thicker, vines and ferns reaching out to grasp the silent runners, the saw grass nicking at their legs. Underfoot, Bolan felt the ground becoming porous, sucking at his feet and threatening to slow him down. The little guy was having greater difficulty, slogging over marshy ground with head bent forward, straining now. Bolan imagined he could hear the other's tortured breathing.

Suddenly the quarry halted, turning back to face the hunter. Bolan saw the blue steel revolver rising in a two-handed grip, tracking onto target, and knew that appearances had misled him in his original assessment of the other's armament. Bolan was forced to take evasive action in a hurry, without breaking stride. He could have drilled the guy before the wobbly track, but elected to wait and see, throwing himself headlong onto the turf, rolling, the Beretta out in front of him and steadied with both hands. The human target was still running, backward now, and trying to adjust for the sudden change in his own target's position when Bolan stroked the Belle's hair trigger twice.

The two sizzling rounds bracketed his target, snapping through the stillness of the swamp and angling for shock effect, to plow into the near undergrowth.

"Drop it," he called softly. "Drop it now!" But the antagonist was stumbling backward, losing balance, tumbling to the ground. And kept on going, down and down, disappearing from view inside the space of an eye blink.

Bolan knew what had happened even before his adversary made the recognition. That "solid ground" was a quicksand bog, and the guy had fallen right into the middle of it.

He was thrashing helplessly, up to his armpits and struggling to stay afloat, grunting wordlessly in grim determination when Bolan reached the bog. The Executioner approached cautiously, noting that his quarry still clung stubbornly to his revolver, holding it above the surface of the mire. Bolan's black Beretta never wavered from the slowly bobbing target as his voice reached out across the intervening space.

"Let's trade," Bolan suggested. "My hand for your gun."

It was an offer that could not be refused. The revolver landed on the moss at Bolan's feet and he retrieved it, noting as he tucked it through his belt that the weapon was a Colt Python .357 Magnum.

A lot of gun, sure, and he was doubly thankful now that its owner had turned up short in the proficiency department.

Bolan crouched down beside the bog, leaning far out above its surface, offering an arm. Small hands reached out and gripped his own, slender fingers locked around his wrist, and he hauled back, putting all his strength into the effort. Slowly, reluctantly, the bog gave up its struggling victim, releasing with a wet sucking sound as Bolan pulled him onto solid ground. Bolan dropped to the ground beside him, pinning him there while patting the muddied fingers for other weapons. Terrified eyes confirmed the evidence of tactile senses as the adversary struggled weakly against the search.

Bolan growled, "Well, damn it," and removed the knit cap to release a spill of honey-blond tresses.

The "adversary" was not a "him"—it was a she, one hell of a she, and Bolan knew instantly the identity of the lovely, terrified, angry young woman.

The swampland was a place of jarring contrast, to be sure . . . beauty interposed with sudden, violent death. The problem for Mack Bolan, at this moment, was where to draw the line on this one.

2

The briefing photo had shown a different girl, in far different circumstances, with hardly a hint of the feminine fire and anger that Bolan could not help but see now. Yet this was Holly Bruce for sure, beautiful and provocative as hell despite the swamp slime clinging to the wet fatigues. Frightened, yes, but she was holding up, presenting Bolan with a bold and defiant front.

And he would have to crack that front, for starters.

Bolan crouched, moved his face very close so that she could not miss the urgent message of the eyes as he quietly cautioned, "Quiet... don't move...don't even breathe."

The girl was mad as hell, and scared as hell into the bargain, but she was no dummy. Her own eyes signaled the quick dawning of understanding, skittering away from his warm-cold gaze almost instantly to warily probe the landscape at their rear.

It had been a long, hard run—with plenty of crashing and threshing about—and in broad daylight. The possibility of danger now was very real, and all too imminent. She lay in a fetal curl in Bolan's strong grasp, their cheeks touching and labored breath mingling in the struggle for silence until he finally announced, "Okay. We're clear."

The girl took a deep breath and let it out with a little shudder as she rolled to her back and allowed the pretty head to rest exhausted in the muck.

"Wonderful," she said, in a voice dragged from somewhere between here and hell. "But who are *we*?"

Bolan found a cigarette, lit it, offered her a drag, which she limply refused.

"My name is Phoenix," he told her simply.

"What are you, a cop?"

He gave her a very small smile, stood up, and softly replied, "Sort of."

Holly struggled to her feet and attacked the slime that clung to her. Hot eyes flashed toward Bolan repeatedly during the process. He smoked and watched, smiling faintly, offering no assistance.

Presently she said, "Sort of a cop, huh? Well, three cheers. That beats the hell out of— I've been screaming for a cop for a damned week!"

Bolan took her small hand and pulled her with him to a better, safer place.

"Relax," he told her. "Someone heard. Your father will be found."

"I've already found him, dammit," she protested feebly. "He's back there."

"Then maybe I would have found him by now, if you hadn't crossed my track."

"I crossed your track!" she spluttered. "That's the damnedest—your track!"

"You sure cuss a lot," Bolan told her, grinning.

And it reached her. He sensed the quick change in her mental atmosphere even before the outward reaction confirmed it. She moved closer, leaning against him ever so slightly for spiritual as well as physical support.

"Thank God you're here," she murmured. "I'm about crazy. Nobody would listen. As if I don't know my own father's habits. He's a workaholic. Never took a vacation in his whole life." And she hesitated. "Who'd you say you are?"

His inflatable canoe was just ahead. Bolan steered her to it as he made the terse reply.

"Phoenix," he told her. "John Phoenix. Washington sent me. Don't worry. We'll find him."

"Phoenix.... Huh, sounds like a code name," she said, coming closer to the truth than she realized. "A phoenix is a bird that rises out of ashes, symbol of eternal life. It's also a city in Arizona. Which one are you named after?"

She was smiling, lightening up, perhaps getting a foot firmly onto the ground for the first time since her grim misadventure began. And she would need that, Bolan knew, before this day was over.

"They named the bird," he replied, "after me. I'm the original million-year-old man."

Holly's interested but still-wary eyes scanned the military figure before the reply came.

"They're sure not making them today like they used to," she said.

A close observer would have noted that Bolan had not yet returned the lady's Colt revolver. There was something in her acquiescence that made him just the slightest bit uncomfortable. She was holding back, without a doubt.

The Executioner well knew that the dangers of the jungle were often concealed in the most alluring packages. Holly Bruce was a wild card, an unknown quantity—and that made for a deadly game indeed.

3

The military commander checked his watch again and turned his eyes skyward, searching. Dusk was lowering over the Everglades, lengthening the shadows of the trees and filling the stagnant air with night sounds of the predators that rule the swamp in darkness. Colonel Charles Rosky hoped the chopper would arrive before they had to use the landing lights.

He had been standing on the helipad for several minutes, and the vigil had done nothing to improve his temper. It reminded him that he was not the sole authority inside the compound, that there were others he must answer to for what went on there.

You want to dance, you have to pay the piper, Rosky thought to himself, scowling in the dusk.

And it had galled him, being forced to call the old man that way, admitting failure. Rosky had been certain that the doctor's stubbornness was taken care of, all ironed out to everyone's mutual satisfaction. Then, overnight, the bastard had turned defiant on them once again, refusing to complete his part of the bargain. Rosky had been all for trying some rough persuasion, the kind that used to get such fine results in Nam, but protocol demanded that he check in with Thurston Ward before taking any action, and the old man had ordered hands-off for the moment. Ward was flying out to handle it in person, instead of trusting Rosky's instincts and leaving it to the professionals.

It disgusted Rosky to have civilians looking over his shoulder, second-guessing him every time he made a command decision. Granted, Ward was better than most—a damn sight better than those sanctimonious assholes in Washington—but he was still a civilian, out of touch with the logic and precision of the military mind. He could never climb inside a soldier's skin and walk around in it, seeing things through the eyes of a man trained to deal from strength and to despise weakness in every form.

Ward was picking up the tab for everything, of course. And naturally he wanted to keep his finger on the pulse of the operation. But as long as he insisted on interfering, meddling, then the eagles perched on Rosky's shoulders meant no more than his captain's bars had meant in Vietnam.

The memory of his Asian wars stirred mixed feelings in the colonel. It was like they said: the best and worst of times. Nam had been a new awakening for Rosky, the peak—and demise— of his career as a regular soldier. He had taken to the jungle like a duck to water, knowing that this war was what he had spent his youth in preparation for. Vietnam provided Rosky with a sense of purpose, a focus. It made him whole.

And he was good at what he did—maybe the best. His success sure caused embarrassment to other less aggressive field commanders. Some of them were jealous of him, and he knew that they had plotted toward his downfall. They did so because he did his job too well. His company brought in the highest body counts, got the choicest information out of captives. They kept the gooks in line, when other companies were being overrun, kicked around like so much rabble. When the generals needed someone to salvage a snafu, they called on Rosky. In the end, when a gang of deskbound pencil-pushers pulled the plug on him to satisfy the liberal press, there was nothing left to do but kiss off eleven years of faithful service and put his skills on the open market.

There had been other wars, other commands, before Thurston Ward sought him out and told him of a grand scheme in the making. Ward had convinced him that he wanted Rosky, needed him, because he hired only the best, and Rosky had accepted it as fact, not flattery. The job brought him a colonel's rank and promises of bigger and better things a few clicks down the road.

But Ward, the civilian, was still pulling all the strings, and Rosky wasn't crazy about some of the company the old man kept.

Ward was the most conservative man Rosky had ever met, even reactionary. No problem there. Rosky had seen the reds up close, and Ward's politics had been a major selling point in his decision to enlist with Warco. Maybe he could stomach all the harebrained radio evangelists who followed Ward around, sucking up to him for contributions. That was all part of the game, the facade. But those others....

They were hard men, rugged in a style unusual for civilians. They came to Ward bearing cash instead of begging for it, and they voiced opinions instead of asking for advice. Worst of all, they treated Rosky like some kind of flunky rent-a-cop.

It rankled.

Ward's choice of friends also made Rosky

nervous. It wasn't like he just fell off the turnip truck. Rosky had seen enough corruption, in Nam and stateside, to know very well the way things worked. But there was something else about these men, an aura of malignancy. It made him feel unclean each time he had to deal with them. They soiled him, diminished him. Rosky had come to hate them for it. He hated them the more because, for the moment, there was nothing he could do about it.

But soon, perhaps....

He heard the chopper coming, drawing nearer. Lifting his eyes, Rosky watched it clear the treetops, circling once around the compound, finally taking up position overhead. It was a big Huey cargo ship, converted to an airborne executive office, painted baby blue with Warco's oil-derrick logo on the tail. Even so, the sight and sound of the chopper never failed to give Chuck Rosky a little thrill of nostalgic pleasure, calling up images of days when he had ridden the flying charger into battle.

The Huey was touching down, and he closed his eyes against the rotor wash, clamping one hand on the bill of his cap and holding it in place. In the freeze-frame of memory, he saw himself emerging, bending low beneath the weight of packs and gear, leading his platoon into another hot LZ. He could smell the jungle, feel it closing in around him, and—

The rotors slowed, blades drooping, and the Huey's cargo door swung back. Thurston Ward scrambled down and out of the chopper, resplendent in a white leisure suit that was almost fluorescent in the dusk. The outfit, combined with his wavy, snow-white hair, reminded Rosky of a mod Kentucky colonel.

And behind Ward, Nicky Fusco was disembarking, quickly regaining his land legs and swaggering across the pad in Thurston's wake. Rosky made a sour face. He had hoped that Ward would make at least this trip without his swarthy shadow. Now he would have to listen while Fusco talked his shit, standing by and saying nothing while the little hoodlum threw his weight around.

Without knowing all the details, Rosky understood that Fusco was Ward's connection with the mob in Florida. So the racketeer's presence in the compound—*Rosky*'s compound—made him uneasy; he didn't like bringing vermin in the house.

At Ward's approach, Rosky stiffened to attention and saluted smartly. The occasion demanded it.

"Good evening, sir," he said.

Ward responded with a stiff salute of his own, unsmiling. Behind him, Fusco arrived in time to witness the military ritual with ill-concealed amusement.

"How's it hangin', General?" the little mobster asked, grinning.

Rosky eyed him coldly, but accepted the handshake. "Mr. Fusco. Welcome aboard, sir."

Fusco's grin faded. "Aboard what?"

Ward smoothly took command. "Any change in the situation, Colonel?" he asked.

Rosky shot another glance at Fusco, wondering if he should speak in front of him. He finally decided that if Thurston didn't mind, to hell with it.

"None, sir," he said. "He's standing firm, but I know we can turn him around if—"

Ward cut him off. "Let me see him, Charles," he said. "I'll have a word with the good doctor before we do anything drastic." A thin smile played across Ward's face as he added, "A simple matter of inspiring cooperation, isn't it?"

It was a gentle slap, but a slap all the same. Ward was reminding Rosky of his place in the pecking order, overruling him—this time in front of Nicky Fusco. Rosky swallowed the humiliation. With a crisp "Follow me," he turned on his heel and set off across the compound, Ward and Fusco trailing.

As they entered the Quonset hut command post, a bull-necked trooper wearing a top-kick's stripes on his sleeve came to attention at his desk.

"Sergeant," Rosky ordered, "have Doctor Bruce delivered to my office."

"Sir."

The trooper was leaving as they passed through a connecting door into Rosky's inner sanctum. Finally on his own turf now, the colonel felt more at ease. He waved Ward and Fusco toward folding camp chairs and lowered himself into the swivel chair behind his own broad desk. Thurston Ward refused the seat and remained standing. Rosky directed his remarks to Ward, pointedly ignoring his companion.

"I believe that when you've spoken to the doctor, you'll agree with me that some constructive force is necessary," he began.

Ward remained impassive. "Maybe so," he granted. "But I want to make that judgment for myself. Any foul-up now could set us back to square one—if it doesn't scuttle us completely."

Nicky Fusco was still wearing that infuriating grin as he put his own two cents in, uninvited. "If you're having problems with the help, I've got a couple of persuaders on the payroll who could make a blind man see the light. I could make a call, and—"

"Forget it," Rosky snapped. "My people are professionals at this."

The grin was still in place, but frosty now. "So are mine, soldier," Fusco answered. "And I guarantee results."

"Listen, Fusco—"

Ward stepped in before things went too far. "Enough," he said, his tone commanding. "Nicky here is only trying to be helpful, Charles," he said, eyes moving on to encompass Fusco in his glance. "Of course, he realizes this is your show, and you're anxious to bring it off without a hitch."

Fusco spread his hands. "Like I said," he drawled, "just tryin' to help."

Rosky eyed him coldly, already forming a rejoinder, but he never got it out. There was a firm knock on the office door, and Rosky let his eyes slide away from Fusco, his voice rising, crisp and curt. "In."

The door opened and the burly sergeant ushered Dr. William Bruce inside, already backing out again before the doctor had a chance to recognize the faces turned to greet him.

Bruce looked bad. His eyes, dull behind the horn-rims, scanned each of them in turn, his mouth setting into a harried scowl. The salt-and-pepper hair looked as if it had been combed with fingers, and carelessly at that. His sport shirt and slacks had obviously been slept in.

Before Rosky could say anything, Ward waved the doctor toward the empty seat and casually parked himself on the edge of Rosky's desk.

"You look like hell, William," he said.

The doctor grunted. "Really? How are prisoners supposed to look?"

Thurston clucked his tongue and put on an injured face. "I'm sorry you disapprove of the accommodations," he said. "But we have a deal, and you're not holding up your end."

Dr. Bruce glared back at his employer. "Forget the deal, *Mister* Ward," he said. "If I had known what you were up to—"

"What am I up to, William?" Ward asked, cutting him off. "Trying to give America another chance? Pulling her fat out of the fire?"

The doctor released his breath in a weary sigh. "Spare me the bullshit. It doesn't wash."

Ward's jaw muscles clenched into knots. Rosky watched as he moved away from the desk, circling the office with exaggerated slowness, stopping at the window. Ward stared outside into darkness for a long silent moment.

He had regained control when he turned back to face the doctor, but his voice was almost cracking when he spoke.

"You may not share my vision, sir," Ward was saying. "Fair enough. I've become accustomed to dealing with short-sighted fools." He was cranking up now, his voice was rising, reaching to the rafters. "I expect your kind of smug self-satisfaction from the bleeding hearts and sycophants, following the Pied Piper down a road to ruin. But I'll be god*damned* if I will let you ruin what I have been planning for a dozen years!"

Every eye was riveted on Ward as he exploded. The tycoon advanced on Dr. Bruce, fists clenched at his sides, his eyes bulging in a florid face. The doctor cringed involuntarily, sinking backward in his chair. One of Ward's fists was rising slowly, trembling, and Rosky could see the veins in his neck standing out like taut cables. Spittle flew from his lips.

"You will *not* stand in my way!" he shouted. "You will *not* . . . . You. . . ."

He stopped, speechless, regaining control of himself with an obvious effort. The fist came down again, unclenching, and Ward's face relaxed, the color fading. When he found his voice again, it had regained the familiar tone of down-home composure.

"Understand me, Doctor," he said. "This project means everything to me. To all of us. We will do anything to see it through. I would prefer to have you as a willing partner, but I will have you—one way or another."

William Bruce was also recovering. He looked Thurston squarely in the eye and said, "You go to hell."

Rosky waited for another outburst, but Ward merely smiled and shrugged. "My associates are anxious to employ some, ah, forceful persuasion," he said. "Your stubbornness is limiting my options. Very soon I may have to let them go to work on you. Or, wh—what's the name of that adorable child? Holly, isn't it?"

The scientist's eyes flickered but he said nothing.

"You have the rest of the night, William," Ward informed him. "I give you that. Do us all a favor and think over what I've said. First thing tomorrow you go back to work...or they do."

And with that, Thurston turned away from Bruce. It was a gesture of dismissal. Rosky punched a button on his intercom, and the sergeant reappeared to claim the prisoner.

"Escort the doctor to his quarters, Sergeant," Rosky ordered. "See to it that he's not disturbed tonight."

"Sir."

Bruce was led away, and the three men were left alone. Thurston Ward settled in the vacant chair and said, "He'll cooperate."

"We're dead in the water if he doesn't," Fusco commented.

Rosky observed, "The shot that marked was the remark about the daughter. That's our best pressure point. Do we have her yet?"

Fusco shifted uncomfortably in his chair as he growled, "Not yet. But the doc doesn't know that."

"You're right, though, Colonel," Ward mused. "The girl is the key." His gaze pinned Fusco. "Let's not miss next time. Let's get her. Indirect threats are one thing, and of course we'll have to use that until something better is in our hands. But once he sees that beloved child staked out in an alligator pit...well, we will see how altruistic and detached the scientific mind can be."

Fusco chuckled.

Ward chuckled, too.

Charles Rosky did not. He was a soldier, not a goddamned pervert. A soldier did what had to be done, sure, but he did not have to look for jollies in that sort of thing. These bastards, here, these.... The military commander could not come up with a fitting appellation for men like them. Ward...well, shit, Ward was a sick son of a bitch, no mistake about that. But a *rich* sick son of a bitch so the soldier would go along with him, to a point. As for Fusco...the guy was pure poison. Rosky the good soldier felt soiled by the association. But he was an ally, dammit, and there was nothing particularly new in warfare about lying down with poisonous allies. Fusco could be suffered for a while, too. But this was going to end as Charlie Rosky's game. No mistake about that. This war was Rosky's war.

"I'll tell you both something." Ward's voice interrupted Rosky's subversive thoughts. "We're close enough that I can taste it now. I will *not* turn back for *any* reason. Charles, if the doctor isn't more amenable come morning—which I frankly doubt—I want him broken. You've got a blank check, as long as he can do his job when you're finished with him. And Nick, I want the girl. Like yesterday. We'll need her as a lever if the doctor proves resistant to persuasion."

Fusco nodded grimly. "You got it, man."

"I hope so. Charles?"

"No problem, sir." Rosky hoped the tone conveyed more confidence than he was feeling.

And he wondered whether that was true, after all. Suddenly, out of nowhere, they seemed to have nothing *but* problems, cropping up on every side. He would have to do something about that, and soon, before Ward began to doubt his wisdom in appointing Rosky to command his grand design. Failure at the finish line was unacceptable, unthinkable.

Hell, it could even be fatal.

4

Bolan crouched in darkness on the enemy perimeter. Waiting. Watching. His eyes tracked the sentries on their rounds, and he got to know the pattern of their movements, the normal interval between appearances at any one specific point along the wire. In their precision, the sentries were predictable. He could have set a watch according to their movements.

His original reconnaissance had shown Bolan that the cyclone fence was not electrified. There were no dogs, no electronic sensors, no security devices of any description. Clearly the hardsite occupants were counting on the Everglades to provide a natural barrier, a murky cloak of invisibility in the lush but shadowy swampland.

And under normal circumstances, sure, it would have been enough. But they had reckoned without the Executioner.

Bolan was in blacksuit, merging invisibly

with the nocturnal shadows of the swamp. His face and hands were darkened with combat cosmetics. The Beretta Belle and AutoMag were in their honored places, backing up the shorty M-16. His harness and the slit pockets of his nightsuit carried razor-edged stilettos, extra magazines, grenades, specially designed garottes. A canvas pouch at his waist contained sophisticated bugging gear, tested and ready for use.

The Executioner was dressed to kill—and hoping that he wouldn't have to. Not on this penetration. He was seeking information first, a better handle on a situation that he did not fully understand as yet. Ideally, he would locate Dr. Bruce and extricate him from the enemy encampment, simply, silently. He would use the arsenal he carried with him only as a last resort.

It was a rescue and intelligence gathering mission first of all. And the less his enemies found out about his presence in their midst, the better.

Bolan breached the chain-link fence with wire cutters, slipped inside. He pulled the flap of fencing shut behind him, and tied it loosely with a couple of twists. It would stand a cursory inspection in the dark, and Bolan was trusting the night and the mossiness underfoot to cover his tracks for the length of time that he would be inside the camp.

Moving swiftly, silently, he confirmed his earlier identification of the generator shack. The lights and voices emanating from two larger Quonset huts told him they were barracks buildings. From their size, and a rapid count of the chemical toilets ranged behind them, Bolan estimated the enemy's strength at forty-five or fifty men.

An army, yeah. But what was its mission?

Turning away from the barracks buildings, Bolan thought he saw a furtive, darting shadow from the corner of one eye. Alert, he hit a crouch and froze, immobile, waiting, every sense alive and tingling. Even in the darkness he felt suddenly exposed, vulnerable. If the sentries found him now. . . .

But there was nothing when he looked again. No voice was raised in warning or alarm. Finally, cautiously, he proceeded on his way. It might have been a shadow after all, perhaps a swamp bat skimming low in search of insects, feeding on the night.

Bolan reached another corrugated metal building, twice the size of either barracks. He played a pencil flash across a darkened windowpane, revealing an array of lab equipment inside. Retorts and beakers, Bunsen burners, racks of test tubes, glittering in the illumination of his flash. Two big refrigerators stood against the opposite wall, flanked by stacks of cages. Captive mice and guinea pigs looked back at him with bright fluorescent eyes.

Satisfied, Bolan killed the flash and moved on, homing on a lighted building that he took to be the base command post. The action, apparently, was there.

Another moment, and the man in midnight black stood beside a lighted window, peering cautiously inside. No one inside there could see him unless he pressed himself against the glass, and his biggest worry was the possible appearance of a sentry deviating from his route. Bolan checked the open ground around him frequently, alternating visual sweeps of the compound with his scrutiny of the office interior.

He recognized the four men present, marking each of them in turn and filing them away. The principals were all accounted for, and Bolan passed over Ward and Dr. Bruce for the moment, concentrating on their two companions.

He had expected Rosky, of course, from his preliminary research, but it was still something of a shock to see the man before him in the flesh. The captain—colonel, he saw now—was like a vision from the past, calling up a period of Bolan's life that he had left behind him long ago.

Rosky had been a regular in Vietnam. A lifer, with exemplary credentials. His aggressive savvy in the field had earned him the nickname of "Can-Do Charlie" early on, but he was not without detractors even then. Critics said that he was brutal with the natives, careless with the lives of men who followed him. Bolan knew enough about the man to doubt the latter charge; as for the former....

Early in his second tour of duty, Rosky faced a general court martial, charged with ordering a "little My Lai" massacre in Trah Ninh province. Harried by reporters, prosecutors hinted that the massacre itself was merely the visible tip of a very ugly iceberg. The captain was acquitted when subordinates stood up to take the heat, but the odor of the case had lingered, scuttling a promising career. Rosky had retired soon after that, and Bolan heard no more of him beyond the things one soldier hears about another through the grapevine. Rosky had become a mercenary, and a good one. There was whispered mention of Angola, Guatemala, the Middle East. He was everywhere and nowhere, earning for himself a different sort of reputation—this time as a soldier of fortune who asked, and gave, no quarter.

They had been formed, Rosky and Bolan, in the same crucible, tempered by the same searing flames, and each of them had turned away from the Asian hellgrounds in the end, to other, private wars.

A similarity, sure. But there was a striking difference, as well. Bolan had done his duty to the utmost, searing terror into the hearts of North Vietnamese and Viet Cong alike, and yet he never lost his humanity; along the way, his caring for the other guy—regardless of age, race, or politics—had earned the Executioner another nickname: "Sergeant Mercy." Rosky took another road, it seemed—he let the war get to him, let it crawl inside his head and build a reeking nest there; he had learned to hate, and he had fallen head over heels in love with war, all at the same time.

A difference, yeah. All the difference in the world.

It was the sight of Thurston Ward's civilian sidekick that gave Mack Bolan his greatest shock as he spied on the group in the command post. The warrior recognized his adversary even before he observed him, pulling up face and name from his mental mug file. But he felt another unsettling flash of *déjà vu* when he looked at the face of the fourth man. It belonged, like Rosky, to a war that was supposed to be long over.

Niccola Fusco—"Nicky" to his intimates—was a South Florida *capo mafioso* with strong South American connections. He had been a street soldier in Miami when Bolan hit the mob's convention there, and he had come out of the ruins in one piece, a survivor. He had moved to Tampa and prospered, away from the Bolan heat and from the competition offered up by Cuban immigrants. Presently, he had a hand in drugs, Caribbean gambling, and the sale of arms to certain "freedom fighters" in the south.

Whatever else his presence in the camp might come to mean to Bolan's mission, it meant trouble and danger for starters.

Ward was doing all the talking as Bolan observed him through the window. William Bruce sat in front of Ward, a bedeviled man struggling for composure. Ward towered over him, his face red with anger or excitement, lips moving rapidly, soundlessly behind the pane of glass.

Bolan extracted a tiny limpet bug from the pouch on his hip. No larger than a shirt button, the transceiver was backed with adhesive that permitted application to any solid surface. Deftly, he pressed it to the lower left-hand corner of the windowpane, counting on the glass to amplify the conversation being held inside.

A receiver, the size of a cigarette pack, was clipped to the front of Bolan's web belt. He plugged the tiny earpiece in, flipped a switch—and smiled as Ward's voice exploded in his ear. A minute adjustment brought the volume to a tolerable level.

"...means everything to me...to all of us," the oil man was telling Dr. Bruce. "We will do anything to see it through. I would prefer to have you as a willing partner, but I'll have you—one way or another."

The doctor stiffened in his chair, no longer cringing, as he said, "You go to hell."

Bolan removed the plug from his ear as Bruce was led away. Thurston Ward had given the doctor the night to think things over. Until sunrise, yeah. Very little time.

The warrior faded back around the corner of the hut. Bruce and his escort came into view. They crossed the compound, heading toward a smaller building that was set apart from the others near the generator hut. When the doctor lagged behind, the burly sergeant took him by the arm and urged him on.

Bolan fell in behind them, discreetly, clinging to the shadows and watching for sentries as he tracked them across the hardsite. He was close enough to touch the sergeant as the guy shoved Dr. Bruce inside his hut and closed the door, fastening a stout lock on the hasp outside.

He was close enough to touch the trooper, sure, but it wasn't part of the plan. Instead, Bolan waited silently in darkness while the sergeant turned away, recrossed the open ground, disappeared inside the lighted office building.

And Bolan moved, sliding out of shadow, edging around to the door of Bruce's prison quarters. A glance through the tiny window showed him Dr. Bruce stretched out on a metal frame cot with one arm thrown across his eyes.

The padlock was a standard model. No problem there. A few seconds' application of the special pick he carried in a slit pocket of the skinsuit, and he would be inside. From there, his options would depend largely on the doctor, and. . . .

A sound. The grating rasp of footsteps close at hand. Bolan turned swiftly, already backing toward the cover of the shadows, but too late.

A trooper, deviating from his beat for no apparent reason, came around the corner of the hut. One hand was scratching distractedly at his crotch, but there was nothing distracted in the eyes that locked on Bolan's crouching figure. If the guy was shocked, he hid it well, lunging for his rifle in a movement that was smooth, fast, thoroughly professional.

Bolan got there first, forewarned of danger in the space of a millisecond, already sliding the Beretta from its armpit sheath before he saw the target. The Belle coughed once, and a 9mm mangler slammed through the sentry's nose and into his brain. The guy folded up and went down without a sound.

Bolan hesitated, glancing from the dead man to the door of Dr. Bruce's hut and back again. He could still take the lock. Only seconds were required. If only. . . .

An unconcerned voice was raised on the perimeter, one guard calling to another. Bolan caught sight of figures moving through the darkness, passing each other on their way to and from the barracks huts. Clearly, it was time for changing of the guard.

He cursed softly, knowing that he might be rediscovered by another guard at any moment. Luck and speed had saved him once, but he couldn't count on them a second time, and the consequences of a running firefight would be disastrous for the doctor and himself.

William Bruce would have to wait, the Executioner decided. He knew from what he had gathered of Ward's conversation that the scientist was crucial to whatever plot was under way here and that his resistance had bought some time for countermeasures. So William Bruce would keep until dawn, at least. But Bolan had to preserve the soft status of this probe. Which meant that he must dispose of the sentry and withdraw to safer ground. The swamp supplied a multitude of hiding places where a corpse could rest in peace—and where a warrior could lay up to plot his strategy.

Bolan threw the sentry's dead weight across his shoulder in the classic fireman's carry. Keeping to the shadows, he turned away from the prison hut and retraced his steps to the perimeter. A delay of several moments was required to let the new, alert patrols pass by, and then he was through the open slit, his cargo borne behind him like a sack of grain.

He would try to connect with Holly Bruce again to let her know that her father was alive and well. Then he had to work a way to spring that man and keep him that way. The rest would wait for the rest. And Bolan knew that "the rest" was going to be sheer hell. It was a worthy foe inside that compound, real soldiers involved in a very real military operation.

American soldiers, dammit, that was the worse part. But they were not, to be sure, soldiers of the same side. And maybe that was the worst part of all.

There were preparations to be made, yeah. Preparations for a rescue.

Sure.

Preparations for Doomsday.

5

Holly Bruce hugged the shadows of the hardsite laboratory, scarcely breathing. She watched the nightfighter's withdrawal from the compound, and shuddered as he bore his grisly burden out of sight. Startled by a passing sentry, she melted deeper into darkness, gripping her revolver tightly in a vain attempt to keep her hands from trembling. Always her eyes returned to the hut that held her father captive.

She had deceived the man called Phoenix with her mock cooperation. And she felt a bit guilty about that... but just a little bit. Whatever Holly might be forced to do or say, she would not be pushed aside, to leave the fate of her father in strange hands.

So she had smiled submissively and given Phoenix a head start on his mission then followed discreetly from a distance. By night, the swamp was menacing in ways that mocked her daylight fears, a place of shifting, rustling shadows, closing on her, threatening. A dozen times she had almost cried out in alarm, almost fired her pistol blindly in the darkness, but she fought the terror and focused on an image of her father, refusing to turn back.

She had watched the man in black as he cut the outer fence and slipped inside the compound, merging with the shadows like a jungle predator. And he was good, Holly gave him that. She followed after him, waiting out the sentries, careful to refasten the flap of fence in place as he had left it.

Once, inside the camp, she thought that he had seen her, but the moment passed and he moved on, allowing her to breathe again. The near miss had shaken Holly, but it also reassured her, built her confidence. Clearly she was better at the game than Phoenix suspected.

She was hanging back beside the lab as the blacksuit peered in through Rosky's office window, watching what went on inside. He pressed something up against the glass, then appeared to put something in his ear, but from a distance Holly could make nothing of his actions. No sound reached her ears, and she cursed the reticence that kept her from advancing to his side.

After seconds or minutes—Holly was losing track of time—the man in black retreated from the window, circling back around behind the

Quonset hut. Holly's heart was in her mouth as she watched her father, followed by a burly soldier, moving wearily across the compound toward another tiny building. She bit her lip as he was pushed inside, the door closed and locked behind him.

And suddenly, Phoenix was there, beside the prison hut, hardly more than a shadow himself. In her concentration, Holly hadn't seen him cross the open ground, following her father and the trooper. He was glancing through the single window of the hut, bending toward the padlock on the door, about to set her father free. Any second now. . . .

And Holly was already moving to join him when the roving sentry came out of nowhere, lumbering into view, upsetting everything. Holly froze, watching, terrified, her mind clicking off the images like some kind of newsreel unwinding in her head.

It was incredible, the kind of detail that the eyes and mind could absorb in crisis moments. She registered the sentry's young-old face, already melting with the shock of recognition, one hand scrabbling absently at his genitals. And she never saw Phoenix make his move, not really. But the image of what happened next would never leave her.

A pencil line of flame silently erupted from

the nightfighter's hand—was that a pistol?—
and the sentry melted backward, sprawling on
the ground. Despite the darkness, Holly saw
his face, or what was left of it, a dripping crimson mask. She knew that he was dead.

If Phoenix hesitated, Holly didn't notice it.
He threw the man across his shoulder, already
moving through the night when voices rose
along the fence. At first, Holly thought they
were sounding an alarm, but she soon decided
it was conversational, unimportant. Apparently no one spotted the burdened warrior as he
returned to the perimeter. No one but Holly
saw him go, as swiftly and silently as he had
come, bearing his cargo of death.

And her first instinct was to follow him, to
put that place behind her, as Phoenix had done,
but Holly held herself in check. If Phoenix was
giving up, so be it. She would not desert her
father now that she had found him. In spite of
any danger, she would free him on her own.

A part of Holly's mind told her that determination was no substitute for planning, but
she was committed now. Boldly, even reckless-
ly, she crossed the open ground, sliding into
shadow when she reached her father's hut.
Nearby, perhaps a yard from where she stood
in darkness, the dead sentry's blood was an
inky puddle on the ground.

Holly took a deep breath, held it, willing her pulse rate back to something like normality. Moving with exaggerated slowness, she circled the hut, peering up and through the single lighted window.

She could see her father, lying on a narrow cot, his back turned toward her. Holly felt the salty sting of tears behind her eyelids as she reached up with trembling fingers, rapping lightly on the windowpane.

No response.

She tried again, and this time her father stirred, turning over, opening his eyes. He sat up, stared at the window, but saw nothing as he looked from light into darkness beyond the glass.

Holly understood. She pressed her face and hands against the pane, watching recognition dawn behind her father's eyes. Surprise gave way to shock, and there was something close to anger on his face as he jumped up from the cot, waving her away. Holly had to make him understand, but before she could communicate by word or gesture, she felt the muzzle of a weapon pressed between her shoulder blades, pinning her against the corrugated steel.

"Hold the pose," a deep voice commanded. "You move, you die."

Holly did as she was told, her face pressed

against the window, looking at her father's anguished eyes. The gun barrel was withdrawn, coarse hands encircled her, patting her down for weapons, lingering for a moment at her breasts in surprise, before moving on to find the pistol in her belt. It was removed, and a hand grasped her by the shoulder, spinning her around.

There were two of them, grinning at her in the darkness. One, a Latin by his looks, held an M-16 leveled at her waist. The other, big and light-haired, had a rifle slung across his shoulder, Holly's pistol in his hand.

"Well, look at this," the Latin said.

"Something for the colonel and his company," the blond man decided.

"Any other weapons?"

The blond one chuckled. "Feels like she's packing a coupla thirty-eights."

They both laughed at that, but Holly was beyond embarrassment. The Latin gestured with his rifle, pointing her in the direction of the lighted office hut. Furious at being taken so, without a fight, Holly led the way across the compound.

She was ushered through an outer door, into what she took for a reception area. The Latin kept her covered with his rifle while his partner knocked on a connecting door, waiting. A familiar voice responded and he passed through, closing the door behind him.

When he reappeared moments later, he left the door open. Glancing at Holly, the blonde jerked a thumb over his shoulder toward the inner office.

"Your turn," he said.

Holly brushed past him, heard the door click shut behind her. Swallowing a sudden urge to run, she looked around the office, taking stock of her surroundings.

Charles Rosky, owner of that too-familiar voice, sat behind a broad desk, smiling at her. Surprisingly, he wore a military uniform, and Holly's gun was on the desk in front of him, muzzle aimed in her direction like a sightless eye. Thurston Ward, the top man in her father's company, was standing at the window, turning now to look at her, arms folded, his face stern, impassive. In a corner to her right, a stranger sat slouching in a camp chair, legs crossed. Holly registered his dark complexion, wavy hair, expensive-looking suit. The man surveyed her with a crooked little smile. His scrutiny made her feel unclean. She turned back to face Ward and Rosky.

"What the hell is going on here?" she demanded. "What is this place? What army is this? What are you doing to my father?"

Ward and Rosky exchanged solemn glances but the other man chuckled and said, "Twenty questions, yet. What a nervy little lady, eh?"

Rosky picked up her pistol and spun the cylinder. "Why were you carrying this, Miss Bruce?" he asked casually.

"It's a jungle out there," she replied shakily. "Or hadn't you noticed?"

"How did you get here?"

"Same way you did."

"What?"

"I followed you from Warco this morning."

Rosky's eyes twitched. The swarthy man chuckled again. Thurston Ward came over to hold a chair for her. "Looks like you got a little lost, though," he commented, eyeing her dishevelment. "You should be more careful, wandering about the Everglades alone. You did come alone?"

She thanked him with her eyes and dropped into the chair. And, boy, she really needed that. Another minute and she would have fallen onto the desk, both legs were trembling so. "What is going *on* here?" she pleaded.

"First things first," Ward replied solemnly, apparently taking over the interrogation. "I'm afraid you are in a bit of trouble, Miss Bruce. You have trespassed upon a top secret government installation. I'm afraid you'll have to explain yourself thoroughly.''

"Nuts to that," she said, sounding a bit more defiant than she actually felt. She was scared to death. "You tell me first why my father is locked up in one of your shacks.''

"It's an isolation hut," Rosky told her. "Your father's own orders.''

"I don't. . . understand.''

"He, uh, was accidentally exposed to a bacteriological agent in his lab.'' The security chief shrugged. "It's standard routine. Your dad simply quarantined himself for 24 hours. Just in case, you know. Don't worry, he's loaded with serum, he'll be okay. This is just a precaution.''

She had a flash vision of her father wildly waving her away through the window of the hut. The whole thing was beginning to make sense. But what about Phoenix?

She told Rosky, "Yes, I saw him through the window. He was warning me away. But why the padlock on the *out*side?''

Thurston Ward took her hand and gently confided, "There could be some brief and quite harmless—but very violent—reactions to the serum, Miss Bruce. Hallucinations and. . . you know. Please take my word that he will be all right. We are much more concerned this moment by your presence here. Can you understand that, Miss Bruce? Can you understand the implications to national security?''

She shook her head to clear it. What the hell...? These men seemed so—but then Phoenix said—but they were *soldiers* and....

"Are you all right, Holly?" Rosky asked quietly.

Thurston Ward replied for her. "She's just frightened and confused, Colonel." He took her other hand. "You must cooperate with us, dear. It is terribly important. Who else knows that your father is here?''

He was so sweet, so fatherly. But Phoenix.... She squeezed both of Ward's hands as she requested, "Could I see some proof? Credentials? Badges? Something?''

Ward dropped her hands and turned away with a broad smile. "Spoken like a true Bruce," he declared warmly. "Would you, Mr. Fusco?''

The swarthy man came out of his chair with a tired sigh, fished a wallet from his breast pocket as he approached her, withdrew a plasticized card and displayed it for her at eye level. It bore an official seal and the words, "Central Intelligence Agency.''

He told her, "I'm Nick Fusco. Mr. Ward's firm is doing top secret work for us. Your father, too, of course. We've had a...problem. Your father's...hurried vacation is, as you guessed, strictly a cover for the work he is doing for us here. Now why don't you cooperate with Mr. Ward? It would be in your father's best interests, believe me."

What an impulsive idiot she had been!

She cried, "My God, who is Phoenix?"

The atmosphere in that office suddenly became positively electric. Rosky asked in an ominous tone, "Did someone come out here with you, Holly?"

"No, but I—"

A commotion at the door took her audience away for the moment.

A man dressed in army fatigues and wearing lieutenant's bars stepped in with a stiff salute and a breathless report. "Penentration Exercise complete, sir. We have a single break at the west perimeter. No hostiles sighted except the prisoner, here. But there is fresh blood in the compound and a sentry is missing."

Rosky quickly pushed the lieutenant back through the door and joined him in the outer office. He banged the door shut behind him but Holly could hear the rumble of excited voices. Mr. Ward lit a cigar and stared worriedly at the closed door. The CIA man sighed and returned to his chair with a bored air that Holly guessed was totally faked.

Good God! What had she done! And she'd witnessed the murder of a U.S. soldier by... oh God, God, God! Did that make her an accessory?

She nearly screamed it: "There's a man out there!"

Fusco quickly came out of his chair and took two nervous steps toward her before responding verbally to that shriek. "Tell it, dammit, tell it!"

She was almost hysterical and she knew it but she could not control her breathing or the strange shrieking sounds she was making. "He said his name was Phoenix!—government sent him!—he killed the soldier and carried him away! I saw it! I saw him do it! Said he wanted my father! Who *is* John Phoenix? *Who is he?*"

"Like in Arizona?" Fusco asked dully.

"Yes, yes, P, H, you know, Phoenix! Who is he?"

"Beats the shit out of me, honey," the CIA man replied, the voice going bored again. His gaze turned to Thurston Ward, who was looking a bit green around the mouth. "Heard of him, Thurz?"

Evidently yes, Mr. Ward had heard of John Phoenix. "Get Rosky back in here," he ordered in a husky voice. "We've got trouble. Big trouble."

For God's sake, Holly could have told them that. She could still see that big jungle cat in her mind's eye, striking with such quick and silent death and then carrying his victim away in the darkness, faster than the mind could even comprehend the act. Like cats can be, though, he had also been very gentle and even protective for a moment, there—for a warm, quiet, even sensuous moment. Oh, it was all so goddamned confusing!

"What could he want from my father?" she asked no one in particular.

But no one answered.

They had their own problem now. That was obvious. She was all alone in the room.

Her father was padlocked inside a filthy hut in a secret military camp in the heart of the Everglades and Holly had been shot at, rescued from quicksand, taken prisoner, then interrogated by the CIA like an enemy spy.

She'd witnessed a murder by a man she'd thought to be an ally, by a man she'd rubbed bellies with and mingled breaths with and could have very easily fallen in love with— probably a damned Russian KGB agent!— and her father had been bitten by his own bug!

Damn! Wasn't it time to wake up, now? Wasn't it?

Unfortunately, no, it was not yet time for Holly Bruce to wake up.

Her nightmare was just beginning.

And it could quite easily prove to be a fatal one.

6

With nightfall, the beauty, always ambivalent, of the Everglades was hidden, obscured by darkness. Now the swamp was merely sinister, a place of furtive sounds and lurking shadows. Every rustling movement in the undergrowth, every ripple on the brackish water, betrayed the presence of a lethal predator. Mack Bolan moved among them, unafraid. He was simply another hunting creature of the night.

Bolan found the bog that Holly Bruce had tumbled into earlier that day. He dumped his human cargo on the grassy lip, and crouching, stripped the sentry of cartridge belt and harness and set them aside for future use. He frisked the lifeless body, seeking anything of value to his mission, but came up empty.

There was no reason for a line soldier to be carrying sensitive material. Rosky was far too professional for any such mistake.

So Bolan would have to gather the intelligence he needed on his own. The hard way. As ever.

He grabbed the sentry by his collar, ignoring the shattered face, and dragged him to the lip of the bog. A gentle thrust and the corpse slipped away like so much laundry down a chute, vanishing by inches in the mire. Bolan automatically closed his ears to the ugly sucking sound as spit-shined boots went under. A last ripple, and the mercenary might have never been at all.

He put that place behind him, shouldering the sentry's gear and moving toward his hidden boat. A portion of Bolan's conscious mind was on alert for any sign of danger, even as the rest of him was reaching for solutions, seeking answers.

Forty-five or fifty men. Professionals. The odds were long, no mistake about it, but the Executioner had faced long odds before. He was not particulary intimidated by the numbers, nor by the fact that his opponents were professionals at doling out sudden death.

To Bolan, the odds were a priority for consideration in the planning stage of any operation. A great warrior could determine probabilities and chart a course of action that would always get him through—provided that he had the necessary information.

It was uncertainty, the unknown variables, that worried Bolan.

Any time a warrior acts from ignorance,

without the proper reconnaissance, without sufficient data for a plan, he courts disaster. Bolan had survived his Asian tours of duty, and his private war against the Mafia, by never leaving anything to chance. If luck—or fate—was a function of the Universe, beyond control, Bolan invariably aimed to help the odds along with superior intelligence and firepower.

So far, on his mission to the Everglades, the Executioner had neither.

He would have to rectify that situation if he hoped to walk away from this one. Every riddle has an answer, every lock a key; all he had to do was find the button and apply the necessary pressure.

Not all that simple, however. The first wrong move, the first mistake in judgment, could be his last. There might never be a second chance to get it right.

First, however, he needed to report good news to Holly Bruce.

His base camp was a camouflaged tent that contained his extra field equipment, and it was dark at his approach. He had cautioned Holly against showing any light that might attract chance patrols outside the hardsite. The chances of discovery seemed slim, but there was no such thing as needless caution in the hellgrounds.

Even considering his admonition, the camp struck Bolan as forebodingly dark and silent. He moored his rubber boat among some cypress boles thirty yards from the solitary tent and disembarked to cross the marshy hummock on foot. His M-16 was at the ready, sweeping the terrain in front of him. Bolan circled toward the campsite like a silent drifting specter of death.

And found it empty.

Holly Bruce was not inside the tent, and Bolan's rapid recon of the area, assisted by the pencil flash, revealed no human presence.

Which could mean anything or nothing. She could have simply decided to go home. Or she could have gone adventuring again, despite Bolan's tutorial on the subject. The latter seemed the most likely, all things considered. She was that kind of person—direct, courageous, willing to stick the chin out.

He took a deep breath. He could understand Holly's action, even as he recognized its foolishness. In other circumstances, other times, Bolan might have done the same himself.

Her impatience and frustration, the urge to take some direct and forceful action, *any* action—he could sympathize with those feelings. But she should have known she was jeopardizing all their lives, the mission, everything.

His mind was sharply focused on the consequences now. At worst, she would get herself
killed and her father at the same time. Too,
she might force Ward into premature execu-
tion of his plan—whatever it was. And of
course the latter possibility was the more important, over any personal consideration for
the girl or Dr. Bruce.

Bolan would do what he could for them,
naturally. But there were no guarantees in this
game.

Well...maybe all was not lost, yet. There
was an outside chance...if he could overtake
the woman before she tried to penetrate the
compound. Nothing here indicated how long
she had been gone, what kind of lead she had.
It was entirely possible, he knew, that she had
already reached the Warco hardsite, already
found a way to breach the wire.

The numbers were tumbling rapidly now.
He would have to make his move without delay.

Bolan was at the tent and reaching for his
satchel of explosives when he heard the sound.
Faint, barely audible, it was like the droning of
a model plane. A hum. He swiveled toward the
sound, flicking off the safety of his M-16 as he
arose from his crouched position. He held his
breath, straining to identify the source.

It was growing louder now, closer, resolving itself into the growl of an engine running over water. The engine noise, baffled and distorted by the swamp's acoustics, seemed to come from everywhere at once, surrounding him and reverberating from the trees.

He was moving toward cover when the airboat exploded into view. Flattening a stand of reeds, it was suddenly upon him, skimming over black water with a heavy-metal snarl. Ducked down in the bow, a pair of riflemen were on alert, eyes and weapons following a searchlight that swept across the hummocks.

Bolan was breaking for the cover of a cypress bole when the searchlight found him, sweeping him with its blinding glare. A warning shout, muffled by the roar of engines, and the gunners opened fire.

And, once again, the hellgrounds had come calling on Mack Bolan.

7

Bolan brought his rifle up, a well-practiced swing, and squeezed off a burst of automatic fire. The searchlight shattered. He caught a glimpse of soldiers covering their faces, burying their heads in instinctive defense. And then the boat was past, rushing wide and tilted, churning up a ragged, shimmering wake with its giant rotor blades.

He dropped behind a fallen log, watching as the pilot made his circuit to line up another strafing run. He saw the airboat tremble, building momentum, then toss itself across the water in an arrow-straight run for the shore. Rapid rifle-fire probed the undergrowth, seeking Bolan's hiding place in a raking pattern. He heard the deadly issue rip through the fabric of his tent.

Bolan drew the silver AutoMag and swung it into target acquisition. Above his sights, the swamp buggy was a hurtling projectile, looming large. The riflemen were etched in silhouette. Flames stabbed from the muzzles of their weapons. The Executioner passed them over, opting for another target, triggering a single devastating round.

And the pilot, riding his tall saddle, never heard the shot that killed him. One moment he was bending to the throttle, high wind in his face, and the next his head had snapped back, driven by 240 grains of hurtling death. The impact spun him on his perch, slamming him back against the rotor cage; an arm slid through the railing and was vaporized in crimson mist.

Without a guiding hand, the airboat continued on its collision course toward shore. Impact was imminent when the gunners recognized their peril, scrambling for the gunwales with half a quick spit left to spare.

The buggy struck a sandbar and the craft was airborne, rotors thrashing empty space. Bolan marked the path of falling bodies, heard a startled cry eclipsed by collision with a wall of hulking tree trunks.

From his vantage point, Bolan scanned the field of this engagement, seeking signs of life. Thirty feet beyond his embattled tent, the airboat lay wrenched and banged-up on its side. Smoke was curling from the silent engine. The night was redolent with fumes from the buggy's ruptured fuel tank.

A crumpled figure lay beside the wreck, awkward in death. A moment, and Bolan recognized the pilot's mutilated body.

His eyes tracked on in search of living targets. He had seen the gunners fall, and lost them in the flurry of the crash. If one or both of them had managed to survive intact. . . .

Bolan left his cover, circling cautiously around the wreckage of the airboat. A calculated risk, sure—and perhaps his only chance, the way things were stacked up, and tumbling.

The Executioner could not afford a lengthy siege.

Sudden movement on his flank, a glint of gunsteel. Bolan spun into the confrontation, big .44 tracking like an alive extension of himself, his trigger-finger already stroking familiar, inevitable metal.

Two weapons fired as one, the AutoMag's thunder eclipsing the banging chatter of an automatic rifle. Bolan was already diving, rolling from a line of fire that ripped the undergrowth apart. He saw the winking muzzle flash and framed it in his sights, squeezed off another round, firing for effect.

The rifleman erupted from his cover, reeling, laying down an aimless, dead-man's screen of fire. A slug from Bolan's autoloader caught him in the chest and dumped him on his back, twitching in the throes of his departure.

One down.

And Bolan found the second gunner by the water, kneeling in some reeds. The guy was dazed, disoriented. He had lost his rifle. From his fall, his left arm dangled limp and useless at his side.

The soldier was watching Bolan through a seeping veil of blood, making recognition of the enemy at twenty feet. His good hand scrabbled clumsily at the flap of his military holster.

The AutoMag arose and was fired. Bolan did not have to aim, nor watch the lifeless body tumble over backward into darkness. It was all over for the mercenary, irrevocably.

But for Bolan, it was just beginning.

He was now back at square one. This was clearly a search party, not a routine patrol, and they had known where to search. The enemies would be on full alert. Even if the sounds of combat had not reached the compound, these guys would soon be overdue for return.

There was no time to lose. Doomsday was about to drop by, invited. First, though, the blacksuited colonel of the night had to touch base with Jack Grimaldi.

The pilot had delivered Phoenix to the Everglades that morning, skimming in low above the treetops with his Sea Stallion helicopter, picking out a landing zone. He had set the chopper down on water, waiting while Bolan offloaded his equipment in the rubber dinghy, then lifted off again, and put the chopper in a tight arc and disappeared beyond the rising crowns of cypress and water tupelo.

But he was waiting now, listening for Bolan's signal. Mack Bolan could visualize his friend sitting in the Stallion's cockpit, eyes straying from his radio receiver only when he had to scan the darkness for potential enemies.

Grimaldi would be waiting, sure, and until hell froze over if it came to it. He had been there for Bolan. Hell, you couldn't have kept the guy away at any price, and he had already proved his worth—if proof was needed—in Bolan's Colombian campaign, riding out a hurricane and hostile ground fire to bring the mission through on schedule. And in Vietnam, 1980s-style, Jack had performed heroically.

Bolan unclipped a compact radio transceiver from his web belt and brought it to his mouth. "Stony Man One to G-Force."

There was a momentary delay before Grimaldi's familiar voice came back at him, sounding tiny and metallic through the small receiver.

"G-Force. Go."

"The numbers are falling, guy."

"Okay. Give me some."

"Just checking you," Bolan demurred. "May need you on short notice, though. Stand by hard."

"I'm always hard," came the terse reply.

Bolan chuckled and told his friend, "I'm going in. If I'm not out by dawn then it's your game."

"Which game?" asked the worried back-up.

"Incinerate," Bolan replied.

"Incinerate?"

"That's affirmative."

"Roger," was the response. "Understand. If I don't hear by dawn, it's fire time."

Bolan smiled at the darkness as he replied, "You got it, pal."

"G-Force standing by," was the laconic rejoiner. "Use me or lose me."

Bolan chuckled and put the radio away. He rummaged through the shambles of his tent, coming up with a heavy O.D. satchel. A last look around the camp, and he retraced his steps to the waiting rubber boat.

This time, although he was opting for a soft probe, he knew he was going in ready for Doomsday, knew that the soft probe might go very hard with a minimum of warning. If he had to fight his way clear of Warco's hardsite, he meant to be prepared.

He reached the dinghy, climbed aboard, and nosed the little craft around, back in the direction of his target. The Everglades and darkness swallowed him.

8

Bolan lay in shadow at the western perimeter of Rosky's camp. The place seemed to be on full stand-by alert, with sentries pacing off the ground on both sides of the fence. Outside, they moved singly and in pairs, shunning light and seeking union with the darkness. Inside the wire, every soldier seemed to be out and moving, armed for combat.

A rifleman was standing guard beside the point of Bolan's entry on his first penetration. The sentry held his rifle at the ready, eyes riveted upon the dark wall of cypress swamp beyond the fence.

Bolan evaded the exterior patrols, passing by them in the darkness like a wraith. He could have picked a number of them off, but right now he was hunting different game. Reaching a point of relative security, he slipped back into the deep undergrowth and raised a pair of night glasses to his eyes.

The Quonset huts and moving figures leaped

toward his eyes, springing into stark relief with an assist from the binoculars. There was no sign of Dr. Bruce or Holly, no trace of Ward or Fusco in his field of vision. Several beats passed before he picked Rosky out, walking away with his back toward Bolan's hiding place, striding purposefully in the direction of his office building. A quick backtrack pinpointed his last stop as a squat hut behind the generator shack. Yellow light was spilling through a window in the door of the half-hidden structure.

Bolan turned on the bugging receiver clipped to his combat harness. He adjusted the volume control, and waited. The limpet bug on Rosky's windowpane, almost certainly still there, undetected, would enable him to continue eavesdropping from even this range.

Like a mouse in Rosky's pocket. Yeah, but without the added dangers of another penetration. Silently, Bolan blessed Gadgets Schwarz for building a half-mile range into the tiny bugs that he had designed.

It was still there, yeah. In Bolan's ear a door slammed shut, rattling the eardrum just a bit. He winced, fine-tuning the volume until the sound of footsteps on floorboards was at a normal level. Tense, expectant, he lay in darkness, listening for an opener to the war in the Everglades.

Rosky banged the office door behind him and turned to face Thurston Ward. The older man was seated at Rosky's desk, kicked back in Rosky's swivel chair, and he made no move to vacate as the troop commander entered. In his corner, Nicky Fusco fiddled with his fingernails, deadpanning whatever emotions may have been working him at that moment. The atmosphere in there was strained, pregnant. Rosky frowned and leaned against the door, hands in pockets, thoughtful.

"So?" Ward asked impatiently.

Rosky growled deep in his throat. "We're on penetration alert," he reported. "The guy better not try us again." He paused and made a face over some unspoken thought before adding, "I sent a patrol to look for his camp. No report back on that yet. How'd you make out with Bruce?"

"He's seen the wisdom of fulfilling his contract," Ward replied heavily. "Already knew we had the girl. Couldn't wait to reaffirm his commitment. But that doesn't mean a damned thing now, Charlie, if this man Phoenix is on our backs. I told you what my man in Washington had to say about that. This is some new, ultra-secret force operating directly out of NSC. They have already done some amazing things."

"We need to get a guy in there," Fusco growled from his corner.

"Don't worry, we will and damned quick," Ward assured the *mafioso*. "But that won't help us tonight." His cold gaze pinned the troop commander to the door. "Tonight I guess it's all in the hands of our military mind."

Rosky returned the cold stare as he replied, "Who is this Phoenix? I have no profile on anyone by that name. Sounds like a zinger, anyway. I need—"

Ward cut in coldly to say, "*Who* is not important at the moment, Charlie. *Where* is important. *How* is important. *When* is important."

"I know all that," Rosky said irritably. "But if I have the who, the rest will be a lot easier. A good soldier knows his enemy. I know nothing about this Phoenix. And I can't just sit here and wait for the son of a bitch to make another move. How many people are out there with him? Is he likely to call in an air strike? What the hell is going on here? That's what I need to know, Mr. Ward, or this military mind is severely hampered."

"We'll have to move it out of here," Fusco declared boredly. "That's the obvious first move. Any street-corner punk could tell you that. They've found our hideout. So. Swish-click. We better damn quick bail out and find another one."

"Or," Rosky said, "we advance the time-table and launch immediately."

Ward sighed unhappily as he pointed out, "Except that we still have no reliable vector. Our friend Bruce has seen to that. What we need now is time. . . just a little more time."

"How much more?" Rosky wondered.

"If he sincerely cooperates now," Ward said with another sigh, "another 36 to 48 hours. The question is—and I'll have to rely on you, Charlie, for the answer—do we *have* that much time?"

"Depends," Rosky replied. He was worried now. "What does Phoenix know? What is he really after? What sort of timetable is he working?"

Ward stood up and went to the window. He peered outside for a long moment, then turned back with a fire in his eye. "You gentlemen know how much I have invested in this. And not just dollars, either. It's a lifelong dream, my very destiny. We must succeed. This country is falling. All the democracies are crumbling—rotten inside, rotten outside. We need that bastion. And by God we shall have that bastion. I don't care what it takes, we shall have it."

Rosky and Fusco locked eyes for a moment. Fusco knew. Sure he knew. Thurston Ward was a loony—a very rich one, to be sure, but a loony nonetheless. Fusco was aboard for the very same reason that Rosky was aboard. They had no share in a lunatic's dream of destiny. They were here simply to ride the dream, to milk what they could from it, then to cast it aside when the casting was best.

Rosky told the maniac, "We'll get your bastion, Mr. Ward."

Fusco, too. "It's going to go, Thurz. The pipeline is in place. This whole hemisphere is ready to flow."

Rosky looked from one of them to the other, brow furrowed. There was a pang of envy at hearing Fusco call Ward by his first name, like his oldest living friend. And deep down, beneath the surface anger and uneasiness, the colonel felt a suspicion. Things were passing between Ward and Fusco, even now, about which he knew nothing, and it worried him.

"Pipeline? What's this all about?" he asked, directing his question to Ward.

The old man smiled, rocking back in the chair—Rosky's chair—spreading his hands in a gesture of innocence. "Economics, Charles," he said. "Nothing to concern yourself about. When you've won a beachhead for us, the civilians take a turn. Financial stability is paramount."

Rosky's voice was stiff, almost brittle, as he said, "I see."

Fusco chuckled like a devil. "Got something in your craw, soldier?" he asked, goading Rosky again. "Don't worry about your budget. There's enough for everybody."

Rosky glared at the man in the corner, but again he was distracted by Ward's voice. It exuded sweet reasonableness.

"Be realistic, Charles," the older man was saying. "There's nothing wrong with, let us say, an enlightened special-interest group. We share a commonality of goals."

"I understand," Rosky repeated.

Ward ranted on as if he had not heard. "Together, we have strength. We can achieve great things. Strike a blow against the menace of creeping socialism. Perhaps a fatal blow, who knows? We can form a power base...a...."

Ward hesitated, one fist raised as he found the others watching him. For an instant he glanced about himself, and Rosky thought he looked disoriented, like a fuzzy drunk waking up in strange surroundings and wondering how the hell he got there.

Suddenly, Ward flashed a dazzling smile,

opened his fist and made a sweeping, throw-away gesture.

"Separately," he pontificated, "we're spitting in the wind. Give it time, Charles."

Rosky remained immobile, then nodded. The air of tension in the room receded to a neutral plane and hung there. Ward stood up behind the desk, and for the first time in their acquaintance Rosky thought that he looked old, very tired. The colonel wondered briefly what in hell he had gone and let himself in for. He quickly put the thought away, avoiding any trace of defeatism.

Ward rounded the desk, passing between Rosky and Fusco on his way to the door. Nicky rose as if on cue, following.

"All we gotta do is turn the tap," Fusco assured Ward. "You got all your financial boys in the pocket, Charlie's got the best damn troop money can buy, and I got the network to flow the feed. Now who's gonna beat a combination like that?"

"Only God," Ward said heavily as he prepared to leave. "Or a man called John Phoenix. I want this Phoenix, Charlie. I want him flying from your flagpole at dawn."

"You'll have him, sir," Rosky promised. "I'll have another talk with Holly if we get no positive from the search. Or maybe I'll send her out with them, next time out. We'll get him."

"But if you don't," Fusco commented, "we better be ready to move at daylight, one way or the other."

"That goes without saying," Rosky replied.

"We're agreed, then," Ward declared. "We move at dawn."

But John Phoenix, at the perimeter, could not wait for the sun. He was already moving and he knew, now, what had to be done.

9

Mack Bolan switched off the miniature receiver and removed the earplug, stowing it inside a slit pocket of his skinsuit. His mind was racing, working overtime to make the pieces fit.

Bolan's mission had confirmed both Ward's status as the doctor's jailer, and the oil man's sponsorship of a private paramilitary force under Rosky's overall command. Nicky Fusco's presence, with the eavesdropped conversation, supplied all the proof Bolan needed of a heavy organized crime involvement in the scheme.

Long miles lay between the Everglades and another steaming jungle, halfway around the world, where Bolan had earned his paradoxical nicknames. Mercy and sudden, violent death—contradictory, but far from incompatible. Sometimes, it was impossible to separate the two in Bolan's world.

It took a large man to carry both names well, and Mack Bolan was beyond compare at the task. But his private, endless war had been a costly one for those who chose to call themselves his allies.

Unbidden, Bolan's mind started ticking off the names and faces of the martyrs who had fallen in association with his cause. Some had known the risks, and signed on willingly; others had been victims of a deadly circumstance, fated for destruction when their paths crossed Bolan's.

Jim Brantzen, plastic surgeon and comrade from Vietnam, who had given the Executioner his new "battle mask" before the turkey-makers overtook him in the sleepy hamlet of Palm Village.

Margarita, the little Cuban *soldada*, tortured and killed on the eve of his Miami massacre, not so very far from where he crouched in darkness at this moment.

In New York, it had been perky Evie Clifford, a lovely loving woman-child with all the world in front of her until her life tragically intersected Bolan's and the enemy reduced her to a mindless screaming cripple.

Peaceful Bruno Tassily had backed Bolan's play against the Jersey guns of Ugie Marinello, and he had been rewarded with a hideous, lingering death.

As had Georgette Chableu, foxy lady fed

and transformed into something less than human by a soulless ghoul named Sal during Bolan's battle for Detroit.

In the here and now, his new war against terrorism had also claimed its casualties, its "turkeys." Ella Hagen and her children, brutalized in their Georgetown home by mobsters working hand-in-glove with Turkish terrorists. The massacred Meos in Mack's return to Vietnam. And Stuart Dunlop, agent undercover, coughing out his life in a Florida hospital, dying to give evidence of something dark and deadly in the works.

Bolan's hand had brought release to some of those who suffered in his cause, dispatching tortured souls to another plane. With love, sure.

And sometimes, the contradiction between death and mercy disappeared entirely. Sometimes it was no contradiction at all.

Objectively, Bolan knew that he could not assume responsibility for everyone who crossed his path, every victim of the terrorist fanatics he was sworn to annihilate. At the same time, he could spare their burden, and when he saw an opportunity to save another human being from torment, he could never turn his back on the chance.

It was that caring, the willingness to go an

extra mile and jeopardize himself, and his mission, for a fellowman in pain and danger, which set Mack Bolan apart. Without the compassion, without the softness underneath the steel, Bolan might have been merely a ruthless engine of destruction, running without a soul, as if out of control.

Softness, yeah.

Mack Bolan was a superior man. His days were not preoccupied with fine philosophy, and yet his every action in the field was determined by a private code of thought and action. He was not religious, but he trusted in the Universe, recognized the never-ending war between Good and Evil. It was his war, and he recognized the grim imperative of victory.

Defeat in battle was a soldier's risk, the chance he took at every turn. Victory was never guaranteed to any man. But a soldier could shape the odds—with courage, the will to live, determination, with a caring for his fellows and a grim refusal to accept any compromise with Evil.

Bolan sometimes thought his path in life had been predetermined for him. Carved out of living stone by the gods or fates—whatever. But the final decision to accept that path, to walk it in the knowledge that there was no turning back, had been his own.

It had never really been a choice at all. He had seen his duty and he had seized it by the throat.

He would not let it go until the job was done.

10

Moving swiftly and silently, Bolan worked his way around the hardsite perimeter, arriving at the northern point where ground gave way to water. The five remaining airboats were all in place, tethered to the shore with nylon lines. Despite of the alert condition of the camp they were guarded only by one man.

Bolan watched the sentry. He was a young-looking soldier, the scars of acne on his sunken cheeks. An M-16 assault rifle hung muzzle-down across his shoulder, and the trooper's attitude told Bolan that he wasn't taking the alert too seriously. His face was illuminated briefly by the flare of a match as he bent to light a cigarette.

While the sentry smoked, keeping his back to the compound and scanning the swamp with disinterested eyes, a shadow moved behind him, circling. Bolan eased into position, approaching from the mercenary's blind side, moving like a stealthy shade of death as he hovered, then crossed open ground. A razor-thin stiletto from a pocket of the skinsuit was ready in his hand.

Bolan stood within an arm's reach as the kid blew final plumes of smoke into the night and flicked the glowing butt into the darkness. His attention was no doubt focused on the dark line of trees across the water. He would suspect no danger close at hand. He was certain of his own immunity from harm.

It was a fatal assumption. One from which the kid would never have a chance to learn.

Bolan had struck. Stepping quickly forward, he enveloped the enemy with outstretched arms. A firm hand was clapped across the sentry's nose and mouth, twisting his head back and baring the soft arch of his throat. The keen stiletto blade flashed over, across and back, opening the jugular and larynx and carotid artery in one lethal sweep, releasing a silent geyser of blood. Bolan held the quivering body upright for a moment, then helped it to the ground, stooping with it, stretching it out on the mossy bank at his feet.

It was a damned shame. . . another senseless casualty of a wrong war, but at this moment Bolan felt nothing but emptiness. He had to be about his business.

He kept his eyes moving constantly, scan-

usual: life and death. The fact that Bolan knew the game was no guarantee of victory whatsoever. Any one of a hundred things could happen while he was inside the camp; any one of a hundred things could go wrong; any one of a hundred reasons for the Executioner to die.

But Bolan did not play that type of numbers. Odds meant very little, in a game like this. The only numbers that mattered now were inside Mack Bolan's head. . . and heart.

11

Bolan moved swiftly across the open compound in a businesslike manner, showing no
obvious attention to the faceless shapes that
passed him in the darkness, nor they to him.

These were soldiers with a job to do and they
were doing it, setting the defenses, checking
out weak points and moving material around.

It was the compartmentalized military mind
that made these men professionals but it also
made them vulnerable to another pro who
knew their ways and how to exploit them.

Bolan went directly to the hut that had been
Rosky's last stop when he was last seen headed
toward the CP. If it held interest for the troop
commander then it held interest also for the
mission specialist who had a job on the pulse-
beat to accomplish here.

A young trooper stood guard at the door.
Bolan checked the kid's combat rig, tightened
it for him, smiled and went on inside.

It was a minimally furnished apartment—

double bed, small breakfast set, campstove and refrigerator, couple of plain chairs. Holly Bruce sat cross-legged on the bed, shoes off, clothed in fresh, oversized fatigues. Her eyes grew noticeably as she recognized Bolan.

He put a finger to his lips and moved on through, checking the place out. She was poiscd for flight at the edge of the bed when Bolan turned back to her.

"Get your shoes on," he quietly commanded.

"I'm not going anywhere with you," she replied in a strangled little voice. "You've got your nerve coming in here like this. One yell from me and they'll be on you like flies on molasses."

He gave her a sober gaze and asked, "Now why would you do that?"

"The jig's up, killer," she said, the voice growing even more hostile. "I told them all about you. They're out looking for you right now."

"Congratulations," he said, the tone cold but not antagonistic. "They found me. Now do you want to spring your dad or don't you?"

Something in his manner seemed to be confusing the girl. Worried eyes flashed from Bolan to the door several times before settling on her own hands. "Something's crazy here," she decided.

"You bet it is," he agreed. "Tell me your version first but make it damn quick. I have things to do and you're just a small part of it."

"They—this—my father was not kidnapped."

"Did he tell you that?"

"Yes, he did. He was exposed to...something poisonous. He's a biochemist, you know. He quarantined himself out here. That's all. Isn't it?"

She was asking *him*. Bolan sighed and dug for a cigarette. He lit it, exhaled noisily, and told the girl, "They worked a number on you, didn't they? Here's the real pitch, kid, straight and quick. These people are trying to produce biological warfare agents. Your dad was sucked into it little by little but finally he saw the light and wanted to get out. They can't let him do that because they need what he knows and there's no time now to shop around for a replacement. They—"

"But this is a U.S. military installation!"

"Like hell it is. It's Warco property, everything on it including the people. If your dad is playing with them again, it's only to save your pretty hide. Believe it. I had an ear on them earlier tonight when they were putting the pressure to him. He told Ward to go straight to hell. That, uh, was before you came stumbling in here to hand them the perfect weapon to hold over him. That's the story. You've got about five seconds to believe it or not. Which will it be?''

"There's a man with CIA credentials. . . ."

Bolan asked her, "How many would you like to buy? I can get them by the gross at fifty bucks per.''

This girl's head was in some sort of crisis, that much was obvious. They'd done a number on her, okay—and probably her father had contributed to that, feeling that her safety depended on it.

How could Bolan hope to counter something like that?

As it was, he did not have to. Where she pulled it from, Bolan could not say—but she sprang from the bed and began donning muddied shoes with only a cryptic little phrase to explain the decision: "It's sensuous, all right."

He told her, "Make that 'perilous' and believe it. Don't open your mouth to anyone. Let me do all the talking."

Bolan took the lady by the arm and escorted her out of there, telling the youth at the door, "Stay put, we'll be back."

As they crossed toward the lab, she whisperingly marveled, "You just tell them what to do and they do it, huh?"

He steered her clear of a couple of troopers who were wrestling a portable searchlight into place and replied, "Sure. First thing a soldier learns is to obey. These are good soldiers."

The girl shivered and moved closer to him. "But they're not for real."

"Oh, they're for real," he assured her. "As good as you'll find anywhere. But Uncle Sam isn't paying their tab."

"This is what they call a paramilitary force, isn't it?"

Bolan did not discourage the quiet exchange. It made them seem more natural, more in place. "That's what it is," he told her.

"I think it's horrible," she said. "How can they do this?"

"Well, they joined the army and learned a trade," he explained. "Now they go where the work is and where the pay is better."

A guy with lieutenant's bars crossed their path, then halted and turned back, staring curiously at the pair. Holly gave him a restrained little wave with fingers only. Bolan ignored the guy completely and went right on talking. "That one right there. West Pointer, if I know my pedigrees. The guy in charge here was known all over Vietnam as 'Can-Do Charlie.' He was a company commander, the best there was until he went a little crazy. Happened to a lot of them in Nam. It was a crazy war.''

"They're all crazy," the girl commented nervously.

"Not," Bolan said lightly, "as long as the world stays divided between us and them. Some wars are very necessary, the only alternative to slavery or something worse. One of life's little paradoxes—if you're not willing to die for something, it's probably not worth having. Or to kill for something."

She shivered again and moved just a little bit away. "I saw you kill tonight," she confided.

"That's okay," he replied soberly. "I saw you try to kill, tonight, and I was on the deadly end of it."

"That was different," she protested.

"It's different every time," he told her, and that was all he had to say about that. They were approaching the lab. "I'll wait outside," he told her. "Bring your dad out. If he's under guard, send the guard out first. Tell him 'the captain' wants to see him."

Nice thing about this kid—she had a quick mind. You did not need to spell the words for her. She moved on ahead of Bolan and entered the lab.

A moment later, another young soldier with a holstered side arm stepped outside with an expectant face.

Bolan tried to live up to that air of expectation. "Go draw a combat rifle," he commanded. "Then report to the detail leader on the west perimeter."

"Sir, I was told to stay with—"

"It's countermanded. No more soft berths tonight, soldier. On the double, now."

The guy tossed a jaunty salute and double-timed away from there. Bruce and the girl emerged almost instantly, arm in arm. Bolan said to the scientist, "Give me a quick yes or no. Do you want me to take the two of you out of here?"

"Yes," Bruce replied, simply and quickly.

"It could get a little brutal," Bolan warned. "Stay in front of me and walk naturally. Talk. Laugh a little, whatever. Just be natural and stay that way 'til I tell you different. When I do, respond instantly and correctly. Stay alert to my instructions."

"I understand," Bruce replied.

"Start walking. Straight across the compound, directly toward the command post."

The Bruces set off at a brisk pace. Bolan gave them four paces then fell in behind them. Father and daughter chatted breathlessly, quietly—perhaps actually exchanging needed information. Bolan could not hear the words, did not wish to hear them. His ears were cocked to other sources and he was almost totally dependent upon their ability to scan for unhealthy sounds.

They were halfway to the CP when Bolan quietly called forward, "Half left turn. Pass behind the building."

A moment later, "Full right toward the north gate."

A trooper jogged past, headed toward the CP. He tossed a quick, interested look at man and daughter, grinned at Bolan and kept on moving. Bolan did not grin back. He unslung the M-16 and made it ready, then dug inside his O.D. bag, produced an M-203 grenade launcher, mated it to the M-16, dropped in a 40mm flare round.

They were now a bare thirty yards from heaven. Bolan called softly ahead, "When I say go, run like hell straight ahead. Hit the gate and it will open. Take cover in the first boat in line. Remember, it's important, the *first* boat. Don't look back, don't hesitate. Get ready."

Bolan heard but did not see someone moving quickly from the command post. "Hold it there," came the challenge.

"Go!" he quietly commanded his charges. At the same moment he dropped to one knee, swiveled around, and let the flare fly.

Two troopers who had been advancing upon him from the direction of the CP reactively flung themselves to the ground in diverging rolls for cover. Bolan tickled the trigger on the '16 and sent a blazing wreath of tumblers to both sides in a much quicker reaction, marking both targets before either could find comfort anywhere.

The Bruces were halfway home and moving fast.

Bolan sent them a silent prayer followed immediately by 40 millimeters of high explosive lofting toward the command post. The flare found its proper place in the sky and puffed open, releasing brilliance high above the west perimeter. There was a brief, electric moment when Bolan could see startled faces tilted skyward all around that compound, then the HE pummeled the air around the command post and spinning flames leaped skyward.

It was a disciplined force, yes, frozen in the reaction, awaiting orders. Bolan kindly supplied that.

"West perimeter under attack!" he bawled into the night. "Respond! Respond!"

The poor guys did not know what the hell to

respond to, but all seemed game for the game. Automatic weapons began chattering in the distance along the western approach and men were running that way from all over the compound. A confused merc with nothing but a side arm was all that stood between the Bruces and home. Bolan screamed at the guy, "Respond, dammit! I'll cover this side!"

The guy threw a final, despairing look at the two civilians as he ran straight toward Bolan. "Who are those people, sir?" he wailed.

"I've got them, don't worry," Bolan assured the guy's disappearing backside.

Or, rather, boat number one had them. Bolan was less than ten paces out when the proper "response" came. It was Rosky's voice, raised in anger and frustration, that told the tale.

"It's a diversion, dammit! The prisoners!— where are the prisoners?"

Another voice, closer: "Three people at the north gate, Colonel!"

"Well, goddammit stop them! Get some floodlights over there! Stop those people!"

Fat chance, Bolan silently told Can-Do Charlie.

Nothing was going to stop them now.

12

The recovery was too late and too far away.
Bolan already had the giant fan blade accelerating into a blur within its huge protective cage
when the first searchlight beam swept the
bank.

He leaned forward on the stick and kicked
the rudder to send the ungainly boat wallowing
into the shallows. A hail of fire came sweeping
in just as the airboat strained forward and
seemed to rise from the water in quickening acceleration.

"Keep down," he warned his passengers as
the spotlight found them. There was but a
blurred sensing of running and shouting men
pouring through the north gate when he turned
back with a one-hand hold to send 240 thundergrains from the AutoMag straight along the
dazzling beam of light. Darkness again descended.

They were off and running, free and clear,
in their own cozy little environment that

drowned out even the angry crackling of weapons to the rear.

Holly showed him a jubilant face that moved quickly in with a damp kiss. Bolan accepted that, then smiled and cautioned the happy lady, "Better stay down. It's not over yet."

"You are mag-nif-i-cent," she mouthed the words, then kissed him again before returning to her father's side.

Bolan did not know about that. But he was feeling pretty good about the whole thing, for the moment.

One half of the mission's objectives had been achieved. Well...all but achieved. The next step—almost a technicality now—would ensure that achievement and set the stage for the other half.

He released the throttle and kicked the rudder into a settling turn. The backwash swept beneath, cushioning the settlement into a gentle rocking motion. He killed the power and dug for a cigarette.

"What's wrong?" Holly gasped.

"Nothing's wrong," he assured her. "Be still, please. I need the ears right now."

Bolan lit the cigarette. Doctor Bruce quietly requested, "Could I have one of those?"

Bolan passed him his and lit another.

"What are we waiting for?" the scientist wondered.

"Pursuit," was Bolan's terse reply.

The girl said, "Oh." A moment later: "Why are we waiting for it?"

Bolan said, "It's called 'tactics'—or, never give the enemy an even break."

She replied, "Okay. If you say so. I'll never argue with you again, count on it."

He heard it then. The pursuit was on. One... two...three...four engines now firing, four giant fans churning the heavy air.

"They're coming," Bruce announced nervously.

"I was hoping they would," Bolan replied off-handedly, his mind busy elsewhere.

He could see their lights, now—powerful beams piercing the darkness to the rear, weaving and wavering as the boats jockeyed for clearance in the shallows.

The girl gave a nervous little laugh and said, "You're beginning to frighten me again, Mr. Big Bird."

Bolan showed her a sober smile. He said, very softly, "Don't ever be frightened again, little mother." His hand found the radio detonator at his waist. He threw the ready-switch and moved a finger to the firing pin. "Don't look back," he urged the girl. "This won't be pretty."

Can-Do Charlie was fit to be tied. He pranced the bank like a caged animal, seething with impotent rage and cursing everyone in sight. His command officers were trying to get their teams together and into the damned boats and it was all just so goddamn much confusion that it made the troop commander want to puke.

"One fuckin' guy!" he kept raging. "You let one fuckin' guy walk all over us like that! Where's your pride! Where's your self-respect! Get those goddamn things moving, get them out of here! You let that son of a bitch get away with this and we're dead men all of us! Get it moving, goddammit!"

Fusco stood in the background, all boredom gone, a haunted look on his now pasty face. Rosky yelled at him, "What's the matter, Nicky boy? A little firefight too much for the street-corner belly?"

"Don't take it out on me, soldier," the *mafioso* replied in a hollow voice. "I seen plenty of this shit before. But I thought the son of a bitch was dead."

Rosky shoved a trooper toward his boat, then turned disgustedly and retreated to stand beside Fusco. "Which son of a bitch is that?" he tiredly inquired, the rage running out of feed.

"Never mind," the little mobster replied. "It was just a thought. But God, it's right in his league."

This was so much small-talking bullshit to the troop commander. The combat teams were all together now, and in their boats. Rosky raised a stiffened arm, balled the fist, then let it drop. The engines coughed, fired, set up their damnable blast. These boys knew their business. If Mr. Smart-ass didn't know his Everglades like his own front yard, then by God. . . .

"They'll run his ass clear to the Gulf of Mexico," he assured the mobster. Then, musingly, "I can't wait to meet this guy face to face. I just hope they bring 'im back alive."

At that precise moment, something terrible, something awful, something just by God mindblowing unbelievable happened. All four of those fucking boats went to hell at the same time, in one huge mushroom of explosive flame.

The blast deafened Rosky momentarily and sent him rolling along the embankment. Pieces of bodies and all kinds of shit filled the air and rained around him, flaming bodies and droplets of fire mixed together and flying everywhere.

A big fucking fan spun along the embankment like a giant, lethal Frisbee, cutting a trooper in two at the waist and hurtling on to slice open a trucksized gash in the chain-link fencing.

The whole goddamn waterway was blazing

with burning gasoline and the whole shrieking place had turned instantly into a living hell.

Guys were running about on shore with flames consuming them, others cried piteously from the water.

Can-Do Charlie, for a minute there, was back in Nam and reliving all its terrors. It was Fusco who brought him out of it—fucking Fusco, of all people—lying half atop Rosky and grunting with horror. *"Bolan...Bolan... Bolan...."*

What was the dumb shit trying to say?

Can-Do Charlie could not have known, at that moment, that certain mafia-type people who had survived the Bolan wars had their own version of combat flashback. Nick Fusco was of that breed. And Mack Bolan would never be "dead" for men such as these.

Nor would the growing legend of one "John Phoenix" cease to be recited in hushed camp-site whispers by men such as Charles Rosky. It was, after all, a closed circle.

Some wars, yes, were entirely necessary.

13

They were idling along the main channel several miles removed from the scene of carnage,
awaiting a rendezvous with Jack Grimaldi.

The scientist stood at the con beside Bolan,
talking earnestly and unreservedly as his
daughter watched and listened without comment. He had already covered the technical
details of his work for Thurston Ward and was
now responding to pointed "debrief" questions from Bolan.

"How is this bug different from the others
we know about?"

"The major difference is in the vectoring."

"How is that?"

"The vector, or carrier, for this general type
of bacillus is normally a parasite such as fleas,
lice, that sort of thing. The bug cannot survive
outside a host body but is transferred directly
from host to host, infecting and spreading, of
course, as it goes. Bad enough, that way, but
not really too effective as a warfare agent."

"So what is *your* wrinkle?"

"Nothing particularly revolutionary. It's technology, not science. We devised a way to pneumonize the bubonic bacillus for direct vectoring."

Bolan smiled soberly and requested, "In one-syllable words, please, Doctor."

Bruce said, "May I have another cigarette?"

Bolan passed the pack around and even Holly shrugged and took one. "If I'm not dead yet, nothing will get me," she said ruefully.

The scientist lit his cigarette and returned directly to the subject at hand. "In one-syllable words, we hit this thing in the petroleum lab by absolute accident. Trying to find a more effective way to disperse petroleum-eating agents. For oil spills at sea, you know. One of the technicians—Jim Fleishaur, dead now—found one of his experiments out of control one Monday morning, after a weekend absence from the lab. He hit the panic button and destroyed the entire culture. Brought it to me. I'm chief research officer. My job is to investigate such matters. Took me no time at all to correlate his data. I've, uh, had background in CBW for our government.

"I saw right away what Jim had done. Unwittingly, of course. He'd crossed-over and stumbled onto something very deadly. I reported the incident to Thurston and recommended that he make a disclosure to the proper agency in Washington. He agreed to do so.

"Few weeks later I was summoned to a quote top secret unquote meeting in Washington. Seemed legitimate to me, at the time. Thurston went with me. It was all a setup but I had no way of knowing that then.

"The long and short of it is that he conned me into reopening Fleishaur's experiment and expanding it, supposedly under a government contract with Warco. By the time I realized what was happening, the thing had gone too far and was totally out of my control.

"I should have been stronger, I see that now. But Thurston can be very persuasive and even very charming while threatening to destroy everything a man holds dear." The scientist's gaze flickered toward his daughter. He sighed. "I just wasn't that strong. Not until the full truth finally dawned. That charming man is a certifiable psychotic, Mr. Phoenix. In one-syllable words, he's crazy as a loon."

Bolan smiled grimly. "That's all very interesting. But you were going to explain something about the vector system."

"That's the whole wrinkle," Bruce replied quickly. "We get all the effect of bubonic plague. Any medical lab in the world would certify the contagion as such. But it is vectored by oxygen.''

''Oxygen?''

''As a mist. It can be sprayed from the air. That's a catalytic start, you see. Once started—but in thousands, maybe millions of victims, now, all at once—once it invades a host organism, the contagion then spreads as any plague spreads.''

''How does he plan to use it?'' Bolan asked quietly.

''At Grenada, first. Then—''

''At what?''

''Grenada. That's a small island republic just north of Trinidad. Thurston already has a foothold there. Place has been in considerable political chaos since its independence from Britain in the mid-seventies. That's when Thurston put his first roots down.

''The man, as you must know if you're a resident of this planet, is scandalously wealthy. I believe he thought, at the time, that he was going to buy Grenada as his own private little tax haven and set up kingdom come there. It didn't wash. Man name Gairy took over and set up his own little police state.

''Thurston tried for years to buy into that, without success. Gairy was no fool. Must have known that Thurston would own him, too, in damn short order.''

Bolan spurred Bruce on. ''How does he—?''

''I'm getting there. Bear with me. This is an astounding story. Gairy was recently overthrown in a coup engineered by a leftist movement. That really set Thurston's jaw. He's been fuming about that ever since, and he has been quietly infiltrating sensitive areas of the local economy, setting up and financing political resistance, establishing a beachhead, so to speak.

''Now I sincerely believe that the discovery of the bacillus is what pushed him over the edge—a bona fide CBW agent in his grasp. The man was already sick and simply could not handle that sort of power.''

''Are you telling me,'' Bolan softly inquired, ''that he means to loose bubonic plague upon that island?''

''That's exactly what I'm telling you.''

Bolan's eyes twitched at the enormity of the thing but he mouthed a single word: ''Why?''

''Destability. With a double edge. We've also developed a detoxicant. Once the population is practically decimated and the whole place is in chaos, the great humanitarian will descend with his legion of angels to heal the nation and put it back on its feet. But he will not stop there, Phoenix. He cannot. Not with that kind of power at his disposal. A man such as Thurston Ward can never settle for anything less than the most.

"Grenada will become the crime capital of the world. They are already setting up the power structure for that kind of machinery throughout the Western Hemisphere.

"Worse still, maybe—Ward sees himself as some sort of messiah-figure. Within a year, at the least, the world will be seeing bubonic plague in such trouble areas as Cuba, Nicaragua, and wherever leftist philosophies predominate. I would not be surprised to see it pop up in Russia."

"You had the words," Bolan commented quietly. "Certifiably psychotic."

"Exactly. I couldn't—I shouldn't have—look here, Phoenix, you were a godsend. I've been stalling this thing for weeks now, and praying like crazy for miraculous intervention."

"Delaying how?"

"The work was finished three weeks ago. The thing is in place, ready to go. I was preparing my final reports when I discovered, quite by chance, that the U.S. government knew nothing whatever about it. That's when I began prying into the true facts. I didn't know any of this crazy stuff three weeks ago! My God, do you believe for a minute that I would—?"

Bolan halted the suddenly emotional disclaimer with a gently raised hand and an understanding smile.

"I think I know what you've been through," he told the scientist. "And I appreciate your present cooperation. But we're on short time now. Your airlift will be here any moment. Tell me about the delivery system. What is it? Where is it? How do I handle the bacillus once I recover it?"

"Don't worry about the delivery system," Bruce replied. "It's a simple aerosol and can be fitted to any standard spraying apparatus. The bacillus will remain dormant until catalyzed by oxygen or until organically absorbed. The present culture bank, sufficient to initially infect perhaps a million people, is in a pressure bottle in the personal possession of Ward, as far as I know."

"It goes everywhere with him?"

"Not all the time. But if he plans on going anywhere, from now on I guess he'll take it with him."

Bolan dug into his pocket and produced a photo of the dead federal agent. He showed it to Bruce and asked, "Have you seen this man?"

The scientist knit his eyebrows as he replied, "Maybe. Vaguely familiar face. Where would I have seen it?"

"Around here, recently. He died in a Ft. Myers hospital from something resembling bubonic plague."

Bruce's cheek jerked in reaction to that news. "While I was under detention...."

"Yes?"

"I overheard something about a suspected break-in at the test lab near Apoloka. Security had been breached, something to that effect. Perhaps...."

"There have been no human experiments to your knowledge?"

"Oh, sure, but entirely controlled. Volunteers. Well-paid volunteers, I may add. From the military command. That's how we verified the antitoxin."

"Someone breaching security in a lab like that... could he become infected?"

"If he didn't know what he was doing, sure. Did they isolate this victim? Is the situation under control?"

"Seems to be," Bolan replied. "I guess we'll have to wait and see, won't we?"

"I guess so," the scientist nodded grimly. "Maybe I can help, if there's a local outbreak. I know I can. I can duplicate the antitoxin right from the top of my head."

The distant disturbance of airborne rotors could now be faintly heard. "Here comes your transport," Bolan announced. "The pilot will line you in with the proper authorities. Maybe you'd better get that medicine ready and make it available very quickly."

"Be careful with that stuff," the scientist said. "Do not expose it to the atmosphere."

"And what if I want to simply destroy it?"

"Subject Ward's container to a temperature of at least one thousand degrees Fahrenheit. That'll take care of it."

The chopper was now in view. Bolan signaled with the lights.

Grimaldi's voice crackled through the small radio: "Have you in sight, Stony One." He settled onto the water a moment later and cut the engine.

Hopefully this would mark the end of the Bruces' ordeal. The man was guilty of no crime, and certainly no official reports would be filed in this matter. Bolan gave the boat just enough power to start it gliding toward the chopper. Grimaldi was on the pontoon with a tether rope when they came alongside.

"What a boring life," he said, yawning at Bolan.

"Save some for me," Bolan replied, grinning at his friend.

"What are we doing?"

"You're taking these good people home, Jack. Then you're—"

The girl flung herself at Bolan, wrapping him in an emotional but wordless farewell. Bruce shook hands briefly with a weary smile while Bolan was thus engaged, then took Grimaldi's helping hand and made the transfer to the chopper.

Holly left wet tracks all over Bolan's impassive face as she flung herself away, spurning Grimaldi's assistance to clamber into the chopper on her own. She turned back in the doorway to say, in a quavery voice, "Million-year-old man, huh? I like to discuss that with you, some long night."

"Maybe you will," he said, finally showing her a genuine smile.

It shocked her. "It's human!" she declared to no one in particular, then disappeared inside.

"What is this?" Grimaldi wondered.

"It's discreet taxi service," Bolan replied. "Take them someplace safe, Jack. Then get it back here on the double. Fly me some cover above the target zone and respond to my signal."

"Better give me an hour."

Bolan checked his watch as he replied, "You got it, pal. Let's go."

They went, Grimaldi on his "discreet taxi" mission, Bolan toward another rendezvous with certifiable psychosis. This long night was winding down.

14

The Grenada scenario made perfect sense to Bolan. The more he thought about it, the more sense it made—and the more chilling it became to contemplate.

Crazy. Demented logic. But like the doctor said, crazy should not be confused with stupid.

Pushing the airboat through the steamy darkness, Bolan reviewed his working knowledge of Grenada. Positioned in the southern Windward Islands, roughly twice the size of Washington, D.C.—the island was defensible all right, if Ward and Rosky could establish their initial beachhead, commandeer the machinery of government.

And the tiny island nation was accustomed to political upheaval. A British colony as late as 1974, Grenada won independence under unionist and nightclub owner Eric Gairy. There were some, inside Grenada and out, who said that Eric's chief concern with independence was his own desire for freedom from financial supervision, and, in fact, he had used his office as prime minister to openly enrich himself. Within a year, American authorities were describing Grenada as a favorite haunt for fugitives willing and able to buy asylum from the Gairy government.

Natives who protested Gairy's profiteering and his one-man rule were routinely silenced, civil liberties widely suppressed. A hefty tenth of the national budget supported Gairy's hard arm—a secret police force composed of hoodlums from the deadly Mongoose Gang, beefed up by killers imported from the slums of black Africa. Arrests of Gairy's few political opponents were commonplace, and the prime minister was candid in his own assessment of the situation. "Lots of people have tried to get rid of me," he told reporters in the Seventies, "and they are lying in the cemetery."

Some of them, at any rate. Others had survived the round-ups and the purges, meeting secretly and plotting toward the day of Gairy's downfall. It came in 1979, with Gairy on a visit to America, an almost bloodless coup executed by a People's Revolutionary Army.

And the leader of the coup, of that people's army, was Maurice Bishop, regarded by Caribbean neighbors as a leftist moderate reformer. Bishop's New JEWEL Movement—the Joint

Endeavor for Welfare, Education and Liberation—billed itself as a supporter of agrarian reform for the island's landless peasantry.

But there were other, more disturbing indicators.

The New JEWEL's "sweeping reform" had never swept very far, bogging down quickly in a tangle of red tape. The one and only business to be nationalized under Bishop was a bottling plant embroiled in labor disputes.

Bishop was rumored to keep a portrait of Ernesto "Che" Guevara hanging in his home, and in April, 1979, he opened diplomatic relations with Cuba over strenuous American objections.

Fidel Castro strongly denied involvement in Grenada's revolution, but since Gairy's overthrow he had supplied Bishop's government with weapons, technicians, and an airport construction crew.

In mid-August, 1979, Grenada's only newspaper—*The Torchlight*—reported a Soviet naval base under construction on the island, and spoke darkly of other, unspecified military activities. Bishop responded by closing down the paper, thereby effectively blacking out the press in Grenada.

The situation was potentially explosive, for sure. If U.S. diplomats were only quietly concerned, a fanatic super-patriot of Thurston Ward's caliber would be gnawing at the carpet as he watched Bishop's New JEWEL Movement going through its paces. The Grenadan government, openly socialistic, aligned with Castro's Cuba and flirting (at least) with the Soviets, was a natural target for the ultra-rightist's anger and aggressive frustration. If the U.S. had failed to prevent the Red advance in Cuba, Nicaragua, other places, there might be another chance to stop it in Grenada—to turn the tide around.

And Mack Bolan could share the legitimate concern, indeed. He could feel the righteous anger at another native freedom movement twisted and perverted into one more arm of the Soviet pincer movement in Latin America. He could see the danger, feel the heat, and wish that there were easy, quick solutions.

The guy could feel all of that, and still realize that Ward's solution was every bit as dangerous as the original problem itself.

The immediate violation of U.S. neutrality, the danger to Grenada's native population from Ward's "equalizer," all of that was bad enough. But the long view was even more ominous.

If the Warco *putsch* succeeded—and it very well might, with Rosky's troopers and their secret weapon stacked against a relatively small, corrupt and disorganized native military force—Ward would have his own foreign power base, a sovereign island kingdom beyond even the nominal control of American law. Once unleashed, left entirely to his own devices, Ward would constitute a threat to peace and stability throughout the Western Hemisphere.

Almost certainly he could be expected to support or initiate guerrilla strikes against the other leftist governments in the Caribbean, Central and South America. Cuba and Nicaragua were the obvious targets, their enemies already drilling in the same Everglades that sheltered the Warco hardsite.

If some of the broadcasts and publications that he supported were any indicator, the way they blasted American leaders as tools of the communist conspiracy—even the United States itself might be open to attack by terrorists based on the island, once the ball got rolling.

And if Ward's domestic allies were a yardstick for judgment, his island refuge would soon become a haven for reactionary zealots and neo-fascists from all around the world. Fugitive Nazis and Arab anti-Semites, military rulers and Third World colonial strongmen— all of them and more would find a sanctuary and a launching pad in Thurston Ward's New Grenada.

The island's strategic location magnified the potential for disaster. A mere ninety miles off the Venezuelan coast, Grenada was within easy striking distance of Cuba, Miami, Nicaragua. An aggressive government—or independent operators acting with its blessing—could interrupt and jeopardize air and surface traffic throughout the Caribbean.

Take that strategic location, mix in Ward's millions with the wide availability of space-age military hardware—anything from vintage tanks and aircraft to the latest submarines and rocketry—and the Executioner was left with a scenario straight out of *Dr. Strangelove*.

Of course, whatever Ward attempted, any incident he might provoke, from the absurd to the catastrophic, would be laid directly at the door of the United States. No one in Havana, Peking or Moscow would ever accept the story of a rogue American, operating without the sanction of his government. Reprisals would be directed not at Ward and Rosky in Grenada, but directly at America.

Nicky Fusco's position in the Warco triumvirate added yet another dark dimension to the picture. There was established precedent for Mafia connections in Grenada, dating from before independence, and the mob could only prosper under Ward's peculiar version of cut-throat "free enterprise." With a little persever-ance—and a friendly government behind him—Fusco might transform the present tourist econ-omy into something surpassing Havana in the Fifties: a wide-open mecca of gambling, prosti-tution and narcotics.

Fusco was acknowledged, by insiders and federal mob-watchers alike, as a power in the booming Florida drug trade. With a secure base of operations outside the United States, and established pipelines to the Middle East and South America, he could dominate the traffic nationwide.

Hell, why not *world*wide?

Drugs and gambling were the mob's leading money-makers, Bolan knew from grim person-al experience, and with a solid handle on both, Nicky Fusco would become a boss with "legs." From his safe haven in Grenada, beyond the reach of extradition, he could engineer the con-quest and rejuvenation of the Mafia's blood brotherhood in America and across the Carib-bean. Given Fusco's record, and his ever-working imagination, it would be naive to think that he had failed to chart the many possibil-ities.

Granted, the prospect of a Mafia reborn was

insignificant compared to the specter of a world in flames. But it was something that the Executioner could not ignore.

He had invested too much of his life—too much of his *real* life, flesh and blood—in the war against that many-headed dragon to ever let it rise again while he was in a position to oppose it. If Fusco had been in the plot alone, without the aid and comfort of the Warco empire, it would have been cause enough for Mack Bolan to act. As it was, the urgency for action was redoubled.

And the only action, the only appropriate response, was a clean sweep, executed before the Warco hardforce could disperse and strike against an unprepared and unsuspecting target. Already time was running short, the curtain falling, dismayingly inevitable.

It was time to move, with a vengeance. Hesitation was a luxury the Executioner could not afford.

From Mack Bolan's Phoenix Journal:

I've heard it said that there are many different kinds of terrorism. Theoreticians and philosophers have ground out reams of material about the variations: Black versus Red, Left versus Right, radical versus reactionary neo-fascist.

They play their ivory tower mind-games with jargon and statistics, but it seems to me they've missed a vital point along the way.

At bottom, in their guts and in their rotten hearts, where they live and breathe and hatch their plots, all terrorists are brothers. Twins and triplets. When you strip away their surface ideology, flush their master race theories and people's revolutions down the sewer with the rest of yesterday's garbage, they are all the same.

Neo-nazis murder Jews in Vienna or Los Angeles, shouting their "Heil Hitlers" on the way to jail. . . and half a world away, terrorists aligned with Moscow or Peking are firing rockets into synagogues. Catholics killing Protestants in Northern Ireland, and Christians killing Muslims in Beirut, all use the same brand of rifles and grenades, courtesy of common suppliers in the East. The dynamite exploding in a Lisbon church today was bought the week before from Basque separatists in Spain.

And when the smoke clears, you can't tell the dead apart without a program.

There is a brotherhood of terror, and it spans the globe today. Arms and men and hate publications are rerouted and recycled, the mission and the message changing like the seasons, but down deep, where it lives, there is only one message, only one war.

Terror is the message, plain and simple.

Savage Man against the civilizers.

And it makes little difference to his victims in the street whether Savage Man is Marxist, fascist or anarchist. The fact remains that he's a killer and a cannibal, despoiler of everything that's decent and upright and clean.

Sometimes there's a tendency to answer terrorism with a mindless counterterror, to crawl down in the sewer with your enemy and wallow in the slime. If the enemy kills a dozen children, you respond by killing twice as many, and you keep the ante climbing, matching him with every move. Somewhere along the way, without ever noticing, you begin to lose perspective, lose yourself. One day, you look in the mirror and you see your enemy inside there, staring back at you and smiling.

Charlie Rosky is a prime example of the warrior twisted and corrupted. He couldn't face the Cong without resorting to their own terroristic methods, and in time that weakness turned around to meet him coming back. He had the will to fight against the savages, and he certainly had the brains—but he never had the heart.

His failure, the failure of a hundred or a

thousand like him, can't detract from what we tried to do in Vietnam. Soldiers break in every war—some from cowardice, others from their own inability to bend. But soldiers are not the war, the struggle itself. They fight it, win or lose it, and they must live with the results—but the war has a soul of its own, independent of the warriors.

The struggle has a life of its own, good or bad.

I hear apologists for this group or that, trying to excuse the bloody excesses of their side by laying off the blame and finding scapegoats. If the Reds (or the Blacks, the Jews, Christians, cops) hadn't started pushing first, hadn't fired the first shot. . . .

And it all boils down to nothing.

Adolf Hitler posed himself as a messiah in his time. For a handful of malcontents he was the answer to a leftist threat, the solution to depression, inflation, unemployment. If he had a single talent, it was finding scapegoats—building up a government with underpinnings made of prejudice and hatred.

Hitler was irrational, most likely insane—but he was also Evil. In the end, it took a holy war to bring his rotten castle down and clean the filth away. It took a world in flames.

But that was yesterday—my father's war.

Mine is here and now, against a new "messiah," every bit as dangerous and cunning.

The paramilitary right, operating outside established law and justice, is no more an answer to the threat of communism than the Weathermen and Black Liberation Army of the Seventies were champions of civil rights. If anything, the violent reactionaries play into the hands of Moscow and Havana, by attacking legitimate dissenters and providing the real enemy with priceless propaganda mileage.

The brutality of neo-fascist states and vigilante movements provides a tailor-made excuse and justification for the bitter "wars of liberation" favored by the Kremlin. If oppressive states did not exist today, the Soviets would have to create them. As it is, the mania of an Eric Gairy, an Amin or a Trujillo, provides the perfect target for a stage-managed "people's revolution."

And the people have damn little to say about it all.

I began this New War with a determination to eradicate the terrorists of every shade, every stripe. It would be easy to adopt their methods and export the war to a hundred different points around the world, striking at civilians and politicians, meeting terror with terror while the shock troops go about their bloody business unopposed. But you don't eliminate the terror by perpetuating it.

The war I'm fighting now is a kind of surgery. The cancer has been singled out, identified and isolated. All attempts at in-body treatment have been tested and have failed. The only viable alternative is surgery—excision of the tumors when and where they can be found. Yesterday, they surfaced in San Juan, today the Everglades; as for tomorrow....

The war goes on, and it justifies itself. The terrorists must be opposed, the cannibals destroyed—and the civilizers left in peace. Today, there is simply too much at stake for a man with hands and eyes to turn away. If I can stop Ward and Rosky, so be it. If I fail in the attempt....

There's a proverb that says that blood cannot be washed away with blood. For all I know, that may be true.

Sometimes it takes a cleansing fire.

15

Disposal teams had finished bringing out the blackened twists of bodies from the barracks, arranging them in blanket-shrouded rows beside the Warco compound camp command post. Other troops, equipped with makeshift stretchers, were bringing in bodies from outside the northern fence, where mangled airboats had collided and burned to the waterline.

Thurston Ward stood in front of the Quonset housing Rosky's field headquarters, scanning the scene of carnage with narrowed eyes. To his immediate right, the long file of rigid bodies, some of them hideously incomplete, lay beneath a camouflage tarpaulin. And more were being added by the moment. Nicky Fusco stood off to one side, by himself, with a sour expression on his face, hands thrust deep into pockets.

Colonel Rosky was approaching them across the compound, flicking a glance toward the covered line of corpses without breaking stride. He stopped in front of Ward, and Thurston saw that his commander had aged in the past hour. Rosky had lost his military bearing. He had suffered a beating at the hands of strangers, and he was taking it badly.

Rosky scowled at Ward, sparing another glance for the corpses.

"As bad as it looks," he answered. "Forty-five percent of my force is dead or wounded, including five MIA's. We can assume they're dead." He took a deep breath, exhaled slowly, and continued. "The generator's damaged, but we're working on it. All of the airboats—"

Ward cut him off, impatient. "What about our guests?"

"Gone, both of them," the colonel said. "I'm assuming that was the purpose of the raid."

Nicky Fusco ambled over from the sidelines, planting himself beside Ward. He spat onto the ground and muttered, "Shit."

Ward ignored the little *mafioso*, addressing himself to Rosky. "Can we get them back?"

"Negative. Without the airboats...." Rosky let the sentence trail away, unfinished, but he had said everything that needed saying.

Ward's frown was cutting valleys in his face.

"I see," he said tightly. "And how do we stand, defensively?"

Rosky shrugged.

"Difficult to say, without knowing what we're up against," he answered. "After this, we must assume another raid is imminent."

Ward glanced around him at the scene of devastation, trying to keep the disgust from his voice as he spoke. "I agree. Tell me what happened here, Charles."

Rosky shifted his feet uneasily, searching for a semblance of a military posture. His eyes found Ward's and locked on them, but there was something in them that the oil man had never seen there before. Uncertainty, yes, and something else.

A trace of fear.

"Shit." Nicky Fusco half-turned away, sneering. His repetitiveness confirmed the contempt he felt for this "colonel."

Rosky glared coldly at the mobster's silent back.

"I've got twenty dead or wounded, five missing, a barracks and a generator blasted all to hell. That little number with the airboats took some preparation by itself, not to mention the equipment. It was *professional*, all the way," he said.

"Are we certain it's one man?" Ward asked.

Rosky thought that one over for seconds. "I can't vouch for what was waiting outside the wire."

Fusco chimed in again, his voice sneering, goading Rosky. "You can't vouch for much of anything, can you, soldier?"

"Butt out, Fusco." Rosky's voice was tight, on the edge of breaking, his fists clenched at his sides.

Fusco scowled at him. "Ah, screw that," he said. "And screw *you*. Ever since you brought the doctor down here, it's been one foul-up after another. You haven't done a damned thing right, not that I can see."

Rosky bristled. "You could do it better?"

The little mobster spread his hands. "I couldn't do a whole lot worse."

"Dammit, that's enough!" Ward barked, his voice up an octave. "I won't have you fall apart like some kind of rabble. We have a common enemy, and I will *not* permit *anyone* to scuttle everything we have worked for."

Rosky and Fusco were still glaring at each other. They kept their distance, both of them transfixed by Ward. The oil man felt the old familiar redness creeping in behind his eyes. He controlled his temper by sheer force of will, clenching and unclenching his fists in time to the pounding of his pulse. After several moments, when he knew that he was in control again, Ward allowed himself to continue, his tone softening, but only slightly.

"We have suffered undeniable setbacks," he

told them both. "It may be that our plan is doomed already, all our work for nothing. But I will *not* surrender. I will *not* admit defeat until the last bullet of the final battle has been fired! You gentlemen, above all others, should understand my feelings."

And he paused, letting that sink in before addressing himself to Rosky.

"Charles," he said, "it is imperative that we evacuate before this Phoenix has time to strike again. If we can't remove the threat, we must remove the target."

Rosky nodded. "I understand."

"Have your men collect everything of value," Ward instructed. "Be prepared to level all the rest when we leave."

"Affirmative." The colonel stiffened to attention, snapping a salute in Ward's direction before he turned on his heel and marched away.

Thurston Ward watched his field commander go. His mind was already racing ahead, weighing options and alternatives, taking stock of his surviving assets. They had been badly hurt by the enemy, but Ward was unable to admit defeat. Not while life itself remained. Not while there was time, and hope, and....

Rosky was an asset, Ward assured himself. Tough, professional, a battle-hardened veteran. He could take the heat now, as he had done at other times, in other wars. Like many career soldiers, he was limited in vision and imagination to the scope of his profession, but within that scope he was a superior tactician. A survivor, certainly. Ward didn't blame him for the near-disaster at the hardsite, any more than he would blame himself. They were dealing with an unknown factor, an imponderable, beyond what any of them had expected.

Ward glanced over at Nicky Fusco. The little mobster was another asset . . . for the moment. However disagreeable he might be, the man had connections of the sort that could help a fledgling government survive until the major powers started weighing in with formal recognition. Once that came—as it inevitably would, after Ward had proved himself—Fusco and his underworld connections would become expendable. Ward would have his own connections then, and if he chose to perpetuate the business sidelines that Nicky had set up, he would be able to handle it without the *mafioso*'s interference.

When the time came, maybe he would let Rosky off his leash and hand over the mobster as a bonus for services rendered. Charles would enjoy that immensely.

Fusco was speaking now, his voice intruding on Ward's train of thought.

"...hell of a goddamn mess," he was saying.

Ward put on his best pacifying smile, the one he used at meetings of the Warco stockholders from time to time.

"Relax, Nick," he said. "It's salvageable. Charles can pull it out, whatever you might think of him."

"Maybe." Fusco's tone was unconvincing. "I saw this once before, you know."

"Oh?" Ward was suddenly alert, his interest peaked. He turned his full attention to the little mobster, watching him with narrowed eyes.

"I was just a street soldier in Miami at the time, working under Vinnie Balderone. The bosses called a meeting. Everybody came, from all over the country. They were mobbed up at one of them beachfront hotels, and somebody kicked the living shit out of them. Killed fifty, sixty guys, I guess. Bombs and shit flying all around the fucking place."

"One man." Ward's voice had a hollow ring to it echoing the sudden hollowness he felt inside.

"Thing is," muttered the mobster, "the bastard's supposed to be dead. Blew himself up in New York City...."

Ward turned away from Fusco, scowling. He had enough on his mind already without following Nicky on a morbid stroll down memory lane. His military force had been cut in half at one fell swoop, his operations base exposed, his secret weapon still unprepared for delivery on an active target. The fate of some forgotten mobsters in Miami had no relevance for him or for his mission. His crusade.

And it was a crusade, he reflected, in the truest sense. A holy crusade against the forces of darkness that were swallowing his world one god-awful bite at a time. The fight was everything to him now, and he couldn't let go of it. Not while life remained.

Thurston Ward had been born before the existence of an Iron Curtain. Before the red star rose over China and a sleeping giant woke to menace all the East. He had seen his government vacillate and compromise, kissing off the populations of Cuba, Hungary, Czechoslovakia. In his twenties, he had watched America humiliated in Korea, and two decades later the humiliation was greatly worse in Vietnam and Iran. At home, he had watched the Land of Opportunity transformed into a place where every sort of pandering minority took precedence over the bloodline of the founding fathers.

Ward did not necessarily consider himself a racist, fascist, or any of the other labels that the long-haired bleeding hearts applied to him in editorials. You didn't have to hate a man to know that God ordained a place for each of us, and that it was a crime against the laws of nature to forget that place. If he had dealt with men along the way who harbored hate inside themselves, he had done it even as he dealt with Nicky Fusco now—as a means to a very desirable end. Never mind that men and women had been hurt or killed along the way. There was a war going on, and in war, people suffer.

Ward admitted to himself that by contemporary standards his philosophy was radical, extreme. He gloried in the knowledge that from time to time he had helped to strike a blow against the tide of creeping socialism. When others met in living rooms and talked about the perils of the future, Ward had put his money where his mouth was, fighting to preserve that future for another generation of Americans. It had been a dirty fight at times, and it was far from over, but looking back, he did not regret a moment or a dollar spent.

A certain senator had said it best, long years ago, before age and political anxiety had mellowed him, converting him to something like a fuzzy-headed liberal: extremism in defense of liberty was no vice, no crime.

That said it all for Thurston Ward. He had

seen his duty, and applied himself to it with all of the considerable resources at his disposal. He had suffered losses, made some gains, and put some people in positions where they might be able to continue the fight when he was gone. Looking back, he could see that every moment of his life, every action taken, had been leading him, drawing him inexorably to the present moment, to the here and now.

He had another blow to strike, for his brand of freedom, and he knew that nothing could prevent him from succeeding if his faith was strong. Determination was the key to everything in life. The doers won out over every kind of obstacle in the end, and the quitters got plowed under like yesterday's manure. It was the way of the world.

Ward's sacred mission was everything now. It was the focus of his life. No...it *was* his life. He would succeed, or die in the attempt.

It was his destiny.

16

In the final hour before dawn, darkness cloaked the Everglades. Away eastward, across the peninsula, the first flush of morning lightened the horizon, tinging the rooftops of Miami, but shades of night lay undisturbed among the cypress and tupelos. The nocturnal predators still held sway, and the darkness was their friend.

The darkness was a friend, as well, to Mack Bolan. He had abandoned the airboat and moved into striking distance of the Warco camp on foot, keeping to the shadows, his every sense alert to chance encounters with a roving sentry. He stood now in knee-deep water, sheltered by a looming cypress, scanning the hardsite with night glasses.

And he had to give Rosky credit for a quick, professional recovery. His mercenaries had the generator working again—either repaired or replaced, it didn't matter which—and inside the wire the lights were on again. Bolan could make out the men in uniform, bustling around the lab and Rosky's command post. They were busy loading boxes of equipment aboard the waiting Warco helicopter.

Other teams were moving back and forth between the corrugated-metal buildings, stringing wire from hand-held spools. Laying charges, yeah, making ready to blow their bridges behind them when they left. Bolan grinned in the darkness, watching them. Perhaps he could lend them an unexpected helping hand.

Entry to the hardsite would have to be made on sheer unadulterated nerve, he knew. There was no way to finesse it this time, unless. . . .

The shock and confusion of the first strike would have Rosky's men off-balance, shaken by their baptism of fire. In the aftermath of Bolan's initial raid, compensating for their failure, the mercenaries would be preoccupied with their mopping-up assignments. In such an atmosphere, it might be possible for Bolan to move among them briefly.

With nerve. A generous amount of nerve.

From his position, Bolan scanned the fence, his magnified vision settling on the northern gate where he had entered earlier. The twisted, blackened wreckage of the airboats lay half-submerged, like discarded playthings abandoned by a giant maniac child. The long gate was standing open, and nearby the hurricane fence had been slit lengthwise by flying shrapnel. From a shortage of men, and perhaps in the belief that lightning never strikes twice in the same place, the open stretch of wire had been left unguarded.

A savvy warrior knows when to seize upon the errors of an enemy.

Before going in, the Executioner took time to seat radio-controlled detonators in their individual plastic charges. They would all be ready to blow on his silent signal, bringing hellfire once again into Thurston Ward's private fortress.

And Mack Bolan was on the numbers again, playing the ear. It would require all of the master warrior's skill to set the doomsday packages in place. Any false step along the way, any error, would bring the pieces crashing down around him, crushing out his life and any hope of a successful conclusion to his mission.

The Executioner had long been prepared for death. But he would never be prepared for failure.

Bolan left the cover of the cypress bole, wading in toward shore. Something brushed against his ankle under water, slithering between his feet, setting his teeth on edge. The warrior closed his mind to it, taking a firmer grip on his M-16 carbine.

He had a rendezvous to keep with other predators, more dangerous than any swampland denizen.

Bolan reached the grassy bank and scrambled out of the water, pausing there in a crouch to sweep the long perimeter with narrowed eyes. No sentry rose to challenge him, no searchlight pinned him like an insect in its glare. He pressed on, slipping through the open gate and into the compound, an uninvited guest come to join the dance of death.

Thurston Ward stood in front of the Quonset command hut, flanked by Rosky and Fusco. Together they supervised the final preparations for evacuation of the camp, making sure that nothing was forgotten, nothing left to chance.

The loading of the Warco chopper was almost complete, and Rosky's demolition teams were moving in and around the other buildings, setting charges, stringing detonator cable. The men in uniform seemed to have regained a sense of purpose, an organization, which had been lacking in the aftermath of battle. They were beginning to look like soldiers again.

Satisfied with the progress, Ward turned to Rosky, keeping his voice low.

"I want half a dozen men to come along with us, to secure the shipment," he said. "The rest will have to wait for another flight or make their own way out."

Rosky frowned, the wheels clicking inside his skull.

"I don't like the wait," he said. "It's an unnecessary risk. We have skiffs available, and with luck they could make it out to Apoloka by noon."

"Fine," Ward said. "You'll want to accompany them, of course."

Rosky's sudden stiffening, his sidelong glance at Ward, made it clear that no such thing had ever crossed his mind. He thought about an answer, finally settled for, "Of course."

"I'll have vehicles waiting for you," Ward assured him. "There should be no problem."

Nicky Fusco chimed in from Ward's other side.

"I can have a crew waiting when we land in Tampa," he said. "Make sure we don't run into any rude surprises."

Rosky's voice was tight, the anger inside of him suppressed with an effort as he spoke. "That won't be necessary," he said. "My men can handle it."

Fusco grinned. "They didn't handle *this* so well."

Ward intervened before the spat could turn into another shouting match. "I'm sure that any help would be appreciated," he said to no one in particular.

And Nicky's smile was widening, his shoulders rolling in a kind of shrug. "Like I said—"

But he never got it out. Before he could finish the sentence, a thunderous explosion drowned his voice, rocking the compound like a miniature earthquake. Ward and his companions swiveled toward the sound in time to see the laboratory building rise from its foundation, riding a cushion of flame. Almost simultaneously, a secondary explosion tore the smoking shell apart, hurling slabs of twisted metal high into the air.

The shock wave reached Ward, heat washing over him like a draft from hell, the concussion rocking him back. Before his mind could register the scene, another blast ripped the generator hut, propelling the roof skyward. Ward saw a tattered rag-doll figure sailing through the air, then the camp was plunged into darkness—for the second time in as many hours.

In the smoky darkness, explosions were marching around the camp, encircling Rosky's command post in a ring of fire and thunder. Men were charging back and forth across the compound, adding automatic fire to the din of battle, seeking targets in the night. Overcome by a sudden numbness of the soul, Thurston Ward saw his worst nightmare coming true before his eyes.

Across the compound, a tall, shadowy figure emerged from the smoke, muzzle flame stabbing from his automatic rifle. Nicky Fusco jabbed an index finger at the man and shouted, "There's your fucking Phoenix!"

But Rosky was already sprinting away across the hellgrounds, shouting to his men, rallying them against the enemy. Some of the mercenaries stopped their aimless firing, harkening to Rosky's voice, moving up to join him.

And a spray of bullets raked one side of the Quonset hut command post behind Ward, spraying him with shards of lead and steel. He panicked, losing track of Rosky as he made a dash for safety.

As Bolan had suspected, most of Rosky's soldiers were still dazed and dusty from the prior engagement. None of them had challenged him as he moved among them, "inspecting" the buildings, planting charges of his own along the way. Unopposed, he had wired the laboratory, generator hut and barracks buildings in succession, steering clear of the command post where Ward, Rosky and Fusco stood together, supervising the dismantling of the hardsite.

He was leaving the communications hut, following a pair of Rosky's men, when the sixth combat sense alerted him to the fact that he was being watched. He shot a sidelong glance toward the command hut, and found Rosky staring at him, following his every move. And suddenly, yeah, he was all out of numbers.

Renegade or not, Rosky was a consummate professional, and he could pick out a stranger, an infiltrator, even in the darkness and confusion.

It was time to roll for the strike and see which way the pins fell.

Bolan dropped back, letting the mercenary demolition team proceed without him. He sidestepped, moving in among the shadows of the barracks building burned out on his first strike. Unslinging the M-16 from his shoulder, Bolan reached down to key the radio-remote detonator simultaneously.

The wired buildings started to blow, one after another, with a built-in two-second delay between blasts. The rapid-fire detonations ripped the night apart with fire and rolling thunder, bringing hell down upon the heads of Rosky's battle-worn survivors. One team was entering the laboratory when it blew, and the fireball spit them out again. Mangled bodies smoked in the dust. Bolan moved toward the Warco chopper, running under cover of the continuing blasts.

Rosky's troops were charging back and forth across the hellgrounds, dodging the rain of shrapnel and mutilated flesh, firing their weapons at shadows. Men were screaming, falling, and Bolan's automatic rifle joined the chorus, burping out short, controlled bursts at isolated moving targets, toppling one after another.

Two small groups were dueling fiercely across the shattered remains of the generator hut, and Bolan left them to it, moving on. His target was the Warco chopper, and already he could hear the engines whining, warming up, heavy rotor blades slicing through the air, picking up momentum. Bolan wanted to catch them on the ground and nail them there, to contain the threat before it was airborne. Ward might be unaware that his plague was ready for an aerosol dispersion, but his ignorance only made it that much more dangerous to play with.

Before Bolan could reach the target, however, automatic fire began eating up the ground around him, whining past his ears. The random strays were coming in with sudden accuracy, and Bolan whipped around to find half a dozen troopers bearing down on him, Rosky in the lead, the muzzles of their automatic weapons winking at him. One bullet tugged at his sleeve; another traced blood and fire across a thigh. The night was alive with angry hornets humming.

Bolan plunged into a diving shoulder roll and came up firing, sweeping his M-16 in a hellfiring arc, left to right and back again. Two of the mercenaries stumbled as if over invisible trip wires, sprawling into awkward attitudes of death, and the others scattered, fanning out, going to ground. Within a fractured heartbeat, they were firing back at him again.

And Bolan repeated his evasive maneuver—rolling, rising, firing, again and again, matching the hostile fire with his own measured bursts. Each time he rose, fewer weapons answered him, and finally there were none.

He came erect and crossed over to the huddled prostrate bodies of his enemies. Chuck Rosky, the renegade, was lying on his back, ankles primly crossed, one arm outstretched and the other draped across the scarlet ruin of his chest. Bolan was about to turn away when he noted fluttering movement underneath the shredded fatigue jacket and heard a distant moan.

The guy was still alive, yeah. Still clinging to

the tattered shreds of his existence. Bolan went down on one knee beside him, and the dying soldier's head rolled over toward him with agonizing slowness. Glassy eyes faded in and out of focus as they found his own. The voice coming out from between those bloodied lips was a parched whisper.

"Who...are...you?"

"Just a soldier, guy," Bolan told him.

One side of Rosky's mouth turned upward in a knowing smile. The other side didn't follow suit.

"Finish it, soldier."

Bolan stood up slowly, swinging the M-16 carbine around onto target, his finger sliding through the trigger guard. But the light had already gone out behind Rosky's eyes, his head lolling limply on a shoulder.

He was gone, finally, irrevocably, and Bolan wished him well.

The sound from Ward's chopper engines was rising, changing pitch. Bolan turned away from Rosky, toward the helipad, running, knowing in his heart that he was too late.

And the big converted Huey was already airborne, circling and swinging away, climbing rapidly to treetop level. Bolan drew up short, snapping the autorifle to his shoulder, sighting quickly down the barrel at the fleeting target.

His finger found the trigger, tightening. Three rounds rattled off in automatic fire—and then the bolt locked open on an empty chamber.

He lowered the M-16 as the chopper disappeared from sight, screened by the wall of cypress. Unclipping the compact flare gun from his web belt, Bolan angled it skyward and squeezed the trigger, tracing a luminiscent slash across the sky.

17

Jack Grimaldi arrived moments later, his chopper following the path of Bolan's flare like some antediluvian dragonfly in search of prey, rotor wings beating the air. He circled once above the smoldering hellgrounds, then took up station over Bolan's head, hovering, dipping lower, finally touching down. Bolan leaned into the backwash of the rotors, eyes narrowing against the blast.

A hoarse voice was shouting, somewhere to his rear, followed by the crackle of automatic rifle fire. Bolan twisted into a combat crouch, the .44 AutoMag greasing its way into his fist, sliding out to full arm's length extension. In the blink of an eye he made target acquisition and squeezed off a single round, sending 240 grains of death along his backtrack.

The heavy bullet met and mastered yielding flesh, ripping through the human target at a stunning 1,400 feet per second. The startled mercenary was lifted off his feet and swept away, a soaring scarecrow, the autorifle flung from lifeless fingers.

There were other soldiers still abroad, but they were racing for the wire perimeters, seeking sanctuary in the swamp like rats. They posed no threat to Bolan now, and they held no interest for him.

He was already moving toward the waiting chopper, holstering the silver AutoMag, scrambling up and into the cockpit beside Grimaldi. Jack flashed him a welcoming grin, raising his voice in order to be heard above the engines as they lifted off.

"You've been busy again," the little guy was shouting.

"This is half of it," Bolan told him solemnly. "The bird's flown."

"Where away?"

"I marked him west," Bolan answered.

"Roger that."

Grimaldi took the chopper quickly up to treetop level, and Bolan was pressed back into his seat, stomach lurching from the sudden ascent. The little pilot put his whirlybird into a 180-degree turn, leveling off and goosing the accelerator, skimming just above the heads of cypress and water tupelo. The swamp spread out below them like a motley carpet.

And up here it was rapidly growing lighter,

the sun rising at their backs as they bee-lined toward the Gulf. White mist was rising off the Everglades, lending an eerie spectral aspect to the scene.

Bolan snapped a fresh magazine into the M-16's receiver and pulled back the bolt, chambering a 5.56mm round. That done, he raised his eyes to the bubble windscreen again, scanning the wide expanse of misty treetops.

But there was no sign of Ward's converted Huey, no visible trace whatsoever of the prey. Bolan's tension was mounting by the second. His mind was racing, ticking off the alternatives.

He knew that Ward and Fusco could have struck off in any direction of the compass after leaving camp. They might have foxed him. Even now, they could be whirling toward some secret sanctuary in the opposite direction, carrying the plague bacillus with them.

As if his thoughts had communicated themselves to Jack Grimaldi, the pilot glanced over at his passenger.

"Could be they shucked you, Sarge," Grimaldi said. "Might've headed west at first to throw you off."

"It's all we've got, guy," Bolan answered softly.

He didn't even want to think about the grim alternative, the price of failure.

Bolan added, "Ward's carrying the bug with him."

"Terrific. Can he deliver?"

"Without even knowing it."

"Shit."

"You called it, man."

They continued on in silence for several moments more, hope growing fainter with every beat of the gunship's rotors. There was a sudden break in the trees below, and they were passing over a sluggish watercourse, its surface dark and stagnant. Grimaldi glanced down, then snapped his head around in a rapid double-take.

"Hold everything," he snapped, his voice suddenly tight.

"What is it?" Bolan asked.

"Maybe nothing," Jack responded cautiously. "Gimme a sec."

He cranked the chopper around, nosing over into a steep power dive. They were down among the trees in seconds, leveling off at twenty feet above the surface of the brackish water, near enough for Bolan to spot alligators lying on the muddy bank.

And a hundred yards ahead of them, running low and fast with lights extinguished, Bolan spied the Warco helicopter.

"Got him!" Grimaldi cried.

"Let's keep him," Bolan ordered, his voice

exultant, as he tightened his grip on the M-16 carbine.

"We aim to please." Suiting action to his words, Grimaldi opened up the throttle, streaking after the larger aircraft with a sudden burst of speed.

He had already cut the Huey's lead in half when the pilot of the enemy ship spotted them on his tail. Instantly, the Huey seemed to shudder in midair, wagging its tail at them, and then the pilot of the larger ship went into his evasive action.

The Warco ship swung up and out of the tunnel of trees, its flight path curving away to the south, running parallel now to the distant shoreline of the Gulf. Grimaldi followed easily in his lighter, swifter craft, cutting corners and closing the gap even further. Ahead of them, the big Huey zigzagged, dipping and climbing, but Grimaldi clung to its tail like a tenacious airborne bulldog.

Trying a different tack, the Warco pilot throttled back, letting Bolan and Grimaldi close the distance. Swinging wide now, fishtailing, he presented Grimaldi's chopper with a broadside view to port—and Bolan could see that the cargo bay was standing open, a figure clad in camouflage fatigues wrestling an M-60 machine gun onto target.

Grimaldi saw him, too, and put the chopper into a steep banking turn even as a line of tracers spat across their nose. One of the heavy bullets struck a landing skid and ricocheted into space with a metallic twanging sound.

And Grimaldi fell back, taking up his station on the Huey's tail, holding tight. His hand slid down to the little chopper's fire controls.

"That was close," he grinned. "One air-to-air, coming up."

"Delay that," Bolan snapped. "I don't want to blow that plague ship in midair."

Grimaldi eased back in his seat. "What's the play?"

Bolan thought quickly, searching for a plan and finding it.

· "Take me upstairs," he said at last. "I want the gunner's blind side."

"You've got it," Grimaldi told him.

Even as he spoke, the gutsy pilot was hauling back on the chopper's joystick, climbing and accelerating at the same time. Within seconds, they were thirty feet above the Huey, keeping pace, running slightly off-center to the port side.

Bolan swiveled in his seat, craning through the open doorway of the cockpit, bringing the assault rifle to his shoulder and tracking an imaginary target. His plan would require precision work, and there would, in all probability, never be a second chance to make it work. It was now or never.

He raised his voice to make it heard above the roar of wind and engines. "When you're ready."

Grimaldi answered with a grin. "Next stop, ladies' lingerie and hell. . . ."

And the little helicopter nosed over, swooping down to run parallel beside the Warco Huey. The gunner saw them coming, swiveling his big M-60 around to meet them, flame already stabbing from the muzzle.

Bolan stroked the trigger of his M-16, holding the sights on target and riding the recoil. He watched the swarm of tumblers impact on flesh and camouflage fabric, punching through to release a crimson tide. One moment the gunner was leaning over his weapon; the next, he was whipped around, spinning backward through the open cargo bay. In the heartbeat before he plunged on through, his weight propelled the M-60 into a full 180-degree turn. Lifeless fingers on the trigger stitched a line of hot steel-jackets across the inside of the cockpit, and then the lifeless form was airborne, spinning away in free-fall toward the trees below.

And something startling had happened to the Warco chopper. The M-60's final burst had found a target in the cockpit, shearing through flesh, the controls, or both. The big ship was pitching and rolling, drifting, nosing over into a long downward spiral. As it heeled over, Bolan caught a glimpse through the open cargo bay— a fleeting look at Nicky Fusco, pressed back against his seat, mouth ovaled in a silent scream.

Jack Grimaldi was already doubling back when the Huey reached treetop level, bursting on through, shearing off the tops of tupelo on its way toward impact with the marshy ground. Grimaldi circled over the crash scene, hovering, descending through a rising cloud of smoke, giving Bolan a ringside view of the wreckage.

The baby-blue Huey had gone down obliquely, snapping off the tail, its main cargo compartment tumbling the final thirty feet to earth. The two sections—tail and cockpit—lay intermingled in the vines and undergrowth, all twisted together and smoking. Bolan caught a glimpse of fire, spreading slowly in the tangled wreckage, and he knew that it was not enough.

He had to be absolutely certain, sure.

"Burn it, Jack," he said, his voice tight.

Grimaldi hesitated, startled. "Huh?"

"The bug," Bolan told him quickly. "We have to stop it here."

Grimaldi stood the fighting chopper on its

nose, engines screaming in protest, and now his hand was back on the firing controls. The rangefinder locked onto the stationary ground target. Grimaldi lightly touched the trigger mechanism.

Four hot ones rippled out of the helicopter's rocket pods, streaking earthward, and Jack was already taking them out of there as the marshland went to hell beneath their feet. A boiling mushroom of fire was pursuing them, the heat and shock wave thrusting them skyward and away.

Twenty feet above the treetops, they stabilized. Grimaldi regained mastery of the controls. Even there, the air was thick with the acrid smell of burning, pungent, and Mack Bolan knew that nothing could survive that cleansing fire.

He heard Grimaldi's voice, coming to him as if from very far away.

"Home?" the little guy was asking.

Bolan nodded solemnly.

"Home."

Grimaldi put the chopper in a final turn, accelerated, took them up and away from the inferno in the swamp. Bolan closed his eyes and tried to make his mind a blank, but he could not escape the image of the fire, crackling, purging everything before it.

He had traveled far to light that fire, spending lives and blood along the way. Less than twenty-four hours had passed since he first laid eyes upon the Warco hardsite, but for a score of men that day had been a lifetime.

Others would survive—the doctor and his daughter, along with hundreds, maybe thousands of persons he would never know or even see. They slept in peace that morning, or rose with dawn to go about their business, never knowing that their lives had been weighed in the balance. None of them would ever know how close they had come to subjugation and death.

Bolan smiled to himself, letting his mind drift, the vibration of the chopper lulling him into a state of drowsiness. He fought his war so that the thousands, millions of the civilized would never have to know. If they slumbered on, or went about their daily business undisturbed, that was his victory.

Now he was going home.

EPILOGUE

Hal Brognola drew deeply on his fresh cigar and sent a plume of smoke rising toward the ceiling. His big, warm eyes regarded Bolan through the haze.

"The fire was contained by the swamp, with a little help from Park Service rangers," he said. "We're damned lucky that it wasn't in a forest somewhere."

"Or a city," April Rose put in, tucking her legs up under her and moving closer to Bolan in her chair.

Hal nodded somberly. "Amen to that."

They were seated together in the briefing room at Stony Man Farm, where it had all begun for Bolan—was it only the day before yesterday? April sat beside her man, and Brognola faced them both across a polished conference table.

"How are you handling Ward's exit?" Bolan asked the head fed.

"Simple aircraft accident," his friend replied. "A tragic fluke, all so regrettable, etcetera. Nobody's mentioning the hardsite."

"Any feedback on survivors?"

"Bits and pieces," Hal told him. "Naturally, they've gone to ground. We're working on it."

"Rosky was the mover, Hal," Bolan said. "Without him, without Ward, there's no army."

Hal nodded, puffing at his cigar.

"Agreed," he said. "Unofficially, we're satisfied as long as they get lost and stay that way."

April's voice interrupted Bolan's private thoughts.

"I'll bet they're going crazy down at Warco central," she said.

"And you'd win, too," the fed told her, smiling. "The scramble started when the news broke at six A.M. Funny thing about that. . . ."

And he let his voice trail off, without finishing the comment. April urged him on.

"Funny?"

"Yeah," he said. "Ward's only living heir seems to be a daughter, mid-thirties. Spinster."

April made a sour face at him. "Sexist. You'd call a man a swinging bachelor."

Hal grinned back at her. "Naturally," he said.

"Oink."

Bolan smiled, enjoying their playful mood, the refreshing change from tension and life on the edge.

"You were saying?" he prodded Hal.

"Right. I was saying that this bachelorette is into missionary work. As in Africa."

"Poetic justice," April said. "Does she stand a chance?"

Hal nodded.

"A good one," he answered. "She won't get it all, but she'll get enough. Petrodollars buy a lot of CARE packages."

"Good for her." April's tone was serious.

"What about the Bruces?" Bolan asked.

Hal took another pull on the cigar before answering.

"Right now, they're taking in some R and R. Officially, of course, there's no investigation. It's a clean slate. Come the fall, I wouldn't be surprised to find the doctor safely ensconced in a university post."

"And the girl," April asked. "How is Holly holding up?"

"Any injuries were merely superficial," Hal responded, with a nod to Bolan. "She can thank you for that, guy. As far as the emotional contusions...who knows?"

Bolan took April's hand in his and squeezed it.

"She'll make it, Hal," he told the big fed. "The lady's a survivor."

"Well, anyway, it's over," April said. There was no hiding the relief in her voice.

"For now," the Executioner amended.

Hal cleared his throat.

"You know," he said, "the scary thing about it is how close Ward came to pulling it off. If Striker hadn't been available—hell, if he'd been twenty-four hours later...I don't even want to think about it."

And Bolan didn't want to think about it, either. Instead, he thought of all the other terrorists—the faceless, nameless fanatics—who might be working toward completion of their own Doomsday weapons. Already, one of them might be finalizing his preparations, choosing a target, preparing to strike. Even now....

Bolan stopped himself, refusing to follow the morbid train of thought any further. The soldier knew he couldn't second-guess tomorrow. Sufficient unto this day, for sure, was the evil thereof. And tomorrow would have to take care of itself.

Frustration was inherent in the nature of Mack Bolan's private war, and he had learned to live with that, to accommodate it without indulging in self-flagellation. He had chosen the game, or it had chosen him—no matter. He would play the cards as they were dealt to him, with all the martial skill at his disposal.

War everlasting, yes.

This time, his skill had been sufficient.

This time, he had turned the threat around and rammed it down the throat of Savage Man.

And for this moment, for the here and now, it was victory enough.

A profile of the new Executioner

STONY MAN ONE

The following is a declassified report on Mack Bolan

Mack Bolan a.k.a. John Phoenix

After ten years of fighting a one-man war against the Mafia, and evading at the same time what the press called the most intensive police manhunt in history, Mack Samuel Bolan, a.k.a. "the Executioner," ceased to exist. In a new decade he received a top secret presidential pardon, plastic surgery and a new identity as Colonel John Phoenix, Stony Man One, the American government's most lethal weapon against international terrorism.

When the U.S. administration became involved in the transformation of Mack Bolan into Colonel Phoenix, an information profile of "Striker" was prepared. Many aspects of the Executioner's past life and current profile are still secret, but the following report is declassified.

Personal Profile: Mack Samuel Bolan

Mack Bolan has been sought by military authorities, following his desertion from the U.S. Army while on active duty as a penetration specialist in Vietnam, and by five federal police agencies (FBI, SS, Capitol Police, BATF, IRS), the state police of 21 states, scores of local jurisdictions, and the authorities of France, England, Puerto Rico, Haiti, Italy/Sicily, Algeria, Canada, and Mexico. Charges against him have ranged from arson, kidnapping, assault and grand theft. He has been wanted for questioning in connection with over 2000 homicides. But Bolan's one-man war against organized crime—a war which he was winning—is now in the past. A presidential pardon (top secret) followed by the simulated death of Mack Bolan in New York City, plastic surgery, and a new identity (rank: colonel, name: John Phoenix) have sufficed to make him the most effective agent and neutralize any repercussions from his past history.

Mack Bolan is an imposing man, 6'3" tall, weighing 200 lbs, with black hair and blue eyes. He has a strong personality, and definitely "fills a room" when he enters it. Investigations indicate that many people who have met Bolan, or have otherwise been in contact with him, are able to recall his eyes and voice yet are unable to describe his physical appearance. While Bolan descends from Irish- and Polish-American stock, his high cheekbones and a squarish jaw give him an Amerindian appearance. Phoenix indicated that any plastic surgery performed to give him his new identity should include "Neapolitan" features. This request was perhaps due to a desire to pass unnoticed among Italian crime "family" elements.

Prior to Mack Bolan's desertion, he had a highly regarded military career as a master sergeant in Vietnam. After completing high school Bolan enlisted in the U.S. Army at age 17 (underage, with parents' permission). Before his tour in Vietnam he served garrison duty in Korea and Germany. Bolan joined Special Forces and completed parachute, sniper and underwater training at Fort Benning. In Vietnam he led Penetration Team Able on a number of secret and highly successful missions behind enemy lines. He has been decorated with two Purple Hearts, a Bronze Star and a Silver Star.

In Vietnam Mack Bolan received a special commendation for exposing and destroying a black market and extortion ring operated by three American troopers in Tran Ninh Province in 1969. He also earned the nickname

"Sergeant Mercy" for his efforts in assisting civilian women and children caught between opposing arms in the war.

His commitment and loyalty to the U.S. government is beyond doubt. Nevertheless, Bolan's history indicates a tendency for one higher loyalty—to himself. He is known to have a highly individual sense of ethical and moral values, which could only impede his effectiveness as an agent if it were overlooked by his superior officers. This "loyalty" determined his desertion from the military, a decision which was motivated by a family tragedy.

Following an accident which left him unable to work for several months, Mack Bolan's father, Sam Bolan, became involved with the Triangle Finance Company, an organized crime front, and incurred debts of several thousand dollars. Unable to pay, he was subjected to threats, and to violence on at least one occasion. Unknown to her father, Cynthia Bolan allowed herself to be recruited as a prostitute to "work off" her father's debt to Triangle. When the elder Bolan learned of his daughter's action, he became irrational and, on 12 August, shot his wife, two children and himself. Mack's younger brother, John, survived the incident.

When Mack Bolan discovered the elements

which led to the death of his family, he swore an "oath of revenge" against organized crime. His subsequent police record indicates his success in pursuing this goal.

Bolan was highly qualified for his one-man war, not only because of his military training, but because of an unusual personality profile. A psychological assessment notes that Bolan has the ability to kill "methodically, unemotionally and *personally*," without suffering any apparent psychic trauma, and deriving no unnatural elation or excitement from the act of homicide; but he will not shrink from it and tends to regard it as a positive duty to what he understands as the Universe. Although Bolan has shown a "soft spot" toward women and children, he has on two occasions executed adult women in circumstances where he felt justified.

His training as a professional soldier and his rigorous self-discipline during his separation from the U.S. forces have required him to develop a strong mental outlook of absolute physical and mental decisiveness. Bolan/Phoenix is remarkably fit, strong and agile, without any impairment or infirmity, and a physical evaluation notes that he should be capable of maintaining his present level of exertion for many years, barring serious injury.

As it is, Mack Bolan's body bears a history of his private wars in the form of twelve visible gunshot wounds of one sort or another. Four of these scars have no exit holes. There is also a stab wound on his front left shoulder from a stiletto; the wound is rather small, which indicates that his opponent didn't get very far.

As a result of Bolan's professional need for an alert and ready mental attitude at all times, he is extremely particular about his life-style. Phoenix's superiors should be prepared to encounter resistance to any suggestions about changing his style of operation. Bolan/Phoenix is an expert marksman and demolition expert, and he is capable of using, servicing and altering all the basic weapons of the NATO and Warsaw Pact countries. He shoots equally accurately with his right and his left hand. As a sniper, Bolan preferred using the Marlin .444 lever-action rifle, with a 20-power scope for distance; later he was known to use a Weatherby Mark V rifle, bolt action, .460 magnum. His personal weapon is, typically, of his own design: a 9 mm Beretta Brigadier with a custom compact suppressor. He favors the .44 Automag pistol as a secondary side arm. His personal armorer is extending his range of preferred weapons to befit the variety of his official duties.

As a result of a quarter century of military training, Bolan has little social life and does not miss it. He smokes filter cigarettes, enjoys the occasional drink (although never more than two at one sitting, echoing Ronald Reagan's remark to a fellow actor, "You've already had two drinks, why do you want another?"), and does not use drugs or stimulants of any kind, regardless of physical or mental duress.

Bolan's native language is English, although he does speak some Vietnamese, Italian and Polish. While his linguistic skills are limited, he is completely familiar with Morse code and cryptography.

In the past, when given a mission or determining a particular task for himself, Bolan has pursued his goal single-mindedly.

It appears likely that he will choose death before betraying the confidence of the U.S. government.

His history as a fugitive and crusader against organized crime is instructive. He has demonstrated a complete resistance to torture, and even to blackmail and coercive threats to family or loved ones in hostage situations. Such threats, in fact, appear to make Bolan even more determined to accomplish his mission.

Mack Bolan might—repeat might—qualify

as an agent for covert assassination operations. It should be noted, however, that this commendation does not come without cautionary words. His training, high intelligence, knowledge and prowess make Bolan a formidable weapon, but he must be used carefully or not at all. Because of Bolan's highly individualistic ethical and moral value system, any assignment will have to fit within his moral conceptual framework, or he may flatly refuse to participate. Bolan's superiors must be capable of recognizing this limitation and to tread cautiously; not to do so could prove disastrous for everyone concerned.

Mack Bolan is both inclined and equipped to take an eye for an eye; he is fully an adult in his sense of reality. But he is also a forgiving man. He knows how to forgive when circumstances warrant it.

Military authorities have recognized the capabilities of this exceptional man, and Bolan's energies and abilities can be put to the good uses of the U.S. government, rather than wasted as a fugitive of justice who, in any event, appears unbeatable. But one final word of caution is warranted. Any notion that Mack Bolan "The Executioner" is turning over a new leaf by consenting to recruitment as agent Stony Man One is probably wrong.

Given this man's history and in particular his personal loyalty to his own ethical values (which is rare in Bolan's chosen profession), one might well ask whether John Phoenix is leaving behind his personal crusade for justice to join forces with the U.S. government—or is the U.S. government being drawn into joining the Executioner's crusade?

The new Executioner triggers an explosion of acclaim

"Bolan dignifies the American fighting man."
—*Army Times*

"The Executioner returns. The books are action-packed!"
—*Marketing Bestsellers*

"Mack Bolan stabs right at the heart of the frustration and hopelessness the average person feels about crime running rampant in the streets."
—*Dallas Times Herald*

"Lines crackle on every page!"
—*Toronto Star*

"Action and variety!"
—*Independence MO Examiner*

"New publisher, new format, same action! His fans won't be disappointed."
—*The Armchair Detective*

"Far and away the bestselling paperbacks of their kind. The Executioner is big with everybody."
—*Knight-Ridder News Service*

"A publishing phenomenon. Top marks for sincerity and topicality."
—*Village Voice, New York City*

"Bolan is a truly heroic figure in the classic sense. Quintessential man."
—*Slidell Louisiana Times*